Frances M. Wilbraham

The sere and yellow leaf

Thoughts and recollections for old and young

Frances M. Wilbraham

The sere and yellow leaf
Thoughts and recollections for old and young

ISBN/EAN: 9783743367692

Manufactured in Europe, USA, Canada, Australia, Japa

Cover: Foto ©Andreas Hilbeck / pixelio.de

Manufactured and distributed by brebook publishing software (www.brebook.com)

Frances M. Wilbraham

The sere and yellow leaf

THE SERE AND YELLOW LEAF

THE
SERE AND YELLOW LEAF

Thoughts and Recollections for
Old and Young

BY

FRANCES M. WILBRAHAM

AUTHORESS OF 'STREETS AND LANES OF A CITY," ETC.

WITH A PREFACE BY

THE RIGHT REV. W. WALSHAM HOW, D.D.

BISHOP OF BEDFORD, AND SUFFRAGAN OF LONDON

London
MACMILLAN AND CO.
1884

PREFACE.

I AM not sure that my very busy and
hurried life in East London does not
provide a sufficient excuse for breaking
through, in the present instance, a rule
which I have for years found it necessary
to make — that I would not lend my
name to other people's books. If there
is anything which we, in the hot, eager
rush of East London life and thought
and work, need more than aught else,
it is the calm, soothing, restful influence
of such a book as *The Sere and Yellow
Leaf.* It is like going among the moun-

tains and valleys of North Wales, where
I have had the privilege of reading it,
in its quiet simplicity and healthfulness
and refreshment. So when an old friend,
as I trust the authoress will allow me to
call her, described the book to me, and
asked me to say a few words by way of
preface, I found it impossible to refuse,
and so agreed to prove my rule (as other
rules are proved) by an exception. The
purpose of the little book cannot be better
set forth than in words which I quote
from its own pages : " This is no manual
for sickness, but simply an attempt at helpful thoughts as to how best our decline of
life may be made profitable to our juniors "
(p. 147). Many a one, tempted to mourn
over waning powers of usefulness, may
find here hints which may brighten and
invigorate declining years. As in the excellent Society of "Watchers and Workers,"

it is found that the greatest comfort and
blessing that can be conferred on invalids
is to teach them how to be useful to
others, so I am sure it will be the most
precious boon we could bestow upon old
age to show how it may be fruitful of
blessing to those who shall follow after.
Indeed, God gives us all our gifts in trust.
Sorrows and joys, troubles and comforts,
sickness and health—all are meant to
pass on in blessing to others. We may
not receive them selfishly. No doubt
their *first* teachings are for ourselves, but
they are meant to be transitive. It is
the same with age. It has its holy and
beautiful lessons for ourselves ; but it has
also precious things to bestow upon others.
May God bless this book that it may help
many so to use the years of lessening
strength but of ripening experience that
they may guard the young from the subtle

temptations that beset them, and may foster in them those finer and more delicate graces which are the crown and finish of the true Christian life.

W. WALSHAM BEDFORD,
Bishop Suffragan for East London.

PART I.

"To pass from youth in peace, and to achieve
The silver livery of advisèd age."—*Shakespeare.*

*Life's exit—Not necessarily gloomy—A glance at life's
entrance—Strong germs of evil in the child-heart—
Germs of good pointed out by our Blessed Lord—His good
gift of free-will—Sad instances of free-will crushed by
man.*

"I HAVE been young, and now am old"
—a life history in eight words ; capable,
however, like that pure gold wire from
Peru of which we read, of being drawn
out from a limited number of inches to
a thousand yards.

When the melancholy Jaques calls this
world a stage, and its men and women
players in it, he adds, "they have their
exits and their entrances." One exit, as
one entrance, falls to the lot of each of

B

us ; it is in view of that inevitable and not distant exit that I would fain share a few ideas and observations, which, if duly set forth, should be helpful and gladdening, with my fellow-toilers and actors in the perplexing drama of life.

The common-sense, the poetical, and (combining and hallowing both) the religious aspect of this exit, and of the pathway that we approach it by, are full of interest, and may have a peace and a beauty peculiarly their own, akin to the peace and the beauty of long evening shadows following on a hot and garish day.

We will certainly not take splenetic Jaques for our guide, though, like him, we must begin with a glance back at our infancy, at the time when " in the nurse's arms " we entered on act first, scene first, of life's mystery-play. Without such a a glance we hardly appreciate our place in this world's plan ; what we are, and from whose hands we came. Again, since He, who knows all and loves us better than He knows, has deigned to bid us become as little children, should we not try to recall such pure and true instincts as He pointed to, amid the deplorable havoc and evil which have marred that nature?

" How quickly have my years sped!" I hear not a few dear contemporaries exclaim. " On looking back life seems to narrow to a point, to a moment!" Well, it may be so; yet, when I gaze steadily back through the long vista of middle life and youth to first recollections, it is like looking through the big end of a telescope at objects clearly defined, but inconceivably remote, standing out from the dark background of non - existence : the present seems another state of being, the quiet heart and matured brain scarcely recognising the wild stirrings and workings of the child-heart and brain of so long ago.

Juliet's bewildered "I am not I, if there be such an I," not inaptly represents the feeling. Yet the bough that falls into the Thames near its retired and rural source is the same that rides, peeled and battered, on the crest of a wave through forests of stately masts into the German Ocean. The full-grown salmon is identical with the lovely unhatched little creature, whose glittering black eye stares at you under the microscope through its transparent silver shell; the instincts which will one day prompt its strange yearly migrations are dormant, but they are there.

When three years old, I was one of a nursery group playing on the edge of a pool in which one of us suddenly espied a newly-drowned white lamb. I never pass by the spot without recalling the thrill of horror and pity caused by the discovery, yet, like *Waverley*, it is a tale of sixty years ago! Equally vivid is the remembrance, about that time, of the exuberant delight of flying before a foaming spring-tide at Worthing, and being caught and drenched by it. Far less joyous, but as distinct, are my reminiscences—the next winter—of first entering a church, our vast and lofty parish church, not then, as now, nobly restored. A baby brother was to be brought to the font. Perched as I was atop of a tall hassock on tottering knees, my small mind was busy to distraction. There being no sort of proportion or keeping in a child's ideas, memory recalls alike the chill mouldy smell, the grim cross-legged ancestor on his marble tomb, the clerk's stentorian tones drowning those of the aged curate, the black-oak solemn angels high overhead, and alas! the holes in my threadbare and mouse-nibbled hassock. It was all vague wonder and gloom, not without some anxiety for the safety of the passive little one in the curate's hold.

But the child-heart is receptive of far happier and nobler impressions than these, even of an absorbing sense of the nearness of God, not traceable to any outward circumstance. A friend now gone to rest, whose long life was a prosperous one, used to say that by far the happiest hour she could remember was one in early childhood, when, seated alone on a summer's day under a blue sky and within scent of a new-made haystack, she felt her heart overflow with the blissful sense of God's love surrounding her. This picture is as sweet as it is true, but, alas! strange compound that we are, each heart has from the beginning its "wicked corner," as an able brain-doctor phrases it. Indolence, vanity and self-love, greed, fretful discontent, untruth in word and act, passionate anger, find a lodgment there—lurid sparks of evil to be smothered or fanned into a flame. But then there are, on the other hand, love carried out into

reverent and loyal service, obedience, repentance for wrong done, forgiveness of
wrong received, uncomplaining patience.
Thus in the moral, though not in the
natural, world bitter waters and sweet
do gush from the same fountain. These
two summaries form the keynote of our
theme, the chords of which will be struck
separately as we proceed.

Wonderful is the strength of this young
life, which we have just compared to the
spring that gushes up from earth's dark
breast. At first it does but glitter and play
in the morning light, but it has its channel
to work out, and so have we. Here the
metaphor breaks down, as metaphors do,
for the course of the stream depends altogether on outward surroundings of clay,
gravel, or rock ; we, though helped or
hindered by our surroundings, yet have
free-will and power granted to us to work
out our course to the end. It is not on
the mysterious side of free-will that we

need dwell ; we may leave that, with its kindred topics of foreknowledge and fate, to Milton's dark debating society ; neither need we speculate on the peril those run who, using their free-will amiss, find in it

"funesta dote d'infiniti guai."

No, rather let us look on free-will in its brighter aspect as a beautiful gift, enabling us to choose the good, the best, the very best, and intelligently and lovingly to hold by it to the end. This is the only wise or safe course (is it not?) in a world where, as Dr. Johnson tells us, there is so much to be done and so little to be known.

If we wish to realise the charm and value of free-will, we can hardly do better than study Prescott's description of the outwardly blameless Peruvians under their Incas. Hedged in by the most minute and slavish regulations at home and abroad, allowed no option as to their career, they were reduced to the state of automatons by a life of drearily passive obedience.

Or read how the natives of Paraguay lost all spirit and manliness under the absolute though kindly sway of the company of Jesuits. These fathers, reputed stern in Europe, were certainly *very* tender in their dealings with these childlike savages ; but they suffered them not to think or act for themselves, so the Indians sank into passiveness ; and, seeing that the pressure of a feather-bed may be as fatal as that of a sledge-hammer, it followed that when the Jesuits were driven from Paraguay, these hapless ones suffered themselves to be enslaved or massacred unresistingly.

Here is a third instance of the blessing that free-will brings, or rather of the grievous loss its absence entails. After the last siege of Paris and overthrow of the Empire, the convents were suppressed

and their inhabitants dispersed. An
English gentleman, who was an eye-witness
of these transactions, thus describes what
he saw: All the nuns were returned to
their homes but three who had grown old
in the convent and lost sight of all their
friends; indeed, they had ceased to know or
care whether they had any friends. One of
these women had been for full forty years
within the narrowing nunnery walls ; she
had never heard of the outside world, and
so completely had she lost all grasp of
mind that she could not answer the
simplest questions. We tried to converse
with her, but she had no idea beyond the
fixed hours for Vespers, compline, etc., under
which she had lived all those years. When
arrangements for her freedom were sug-
gested to her, she rather chose to creep to
her cell and die there,—a victim to the
destruction by man of God's gift of free-
will by an unbroken rule of silence, and
by quenching all interest in others.

The history of Mahometan fatalism in the East, and that of bigoted Calvinism, now perhaps dying out in the West, teach us the same lesson, and should fill us with thankfulness for our happier lot in being called to glory and virtue at life's beginning, with every incitement to pursue after them, even to its decay and earthly close.

PART· II.

"We all do fade as a leaf."—*Isaiah.*

"The insupportable fatigue of thought."—*Cowper.*

"Il est heureux, ce Monsieur ! il s'aime, et n'a point de rival."

Advancing age—The sere and yellow leaf of metaphor —That of nature—Analogy between them looked into— Deterioration in age, too frequent, imperils our influence with the young—Shows itself in indolence of mind—Self-indulgence—Self-love.

LIFE'S decay and its close—What are the young and the middle-aged to do, and what avoid, in order that these may be edifying and serene ? How best can they guard against the blighting tendencies from without, and the tendencies to disease from within, which, if neglected through our spring and summer-time, canker the autumn leaf ? How best can those graces

which we have enumerated, and shall by
and by return to, be so fostered that, like
the smooth many-tinted foliage of the
maple, they may still remain beautiful in
decay? We will presently go into these
questions in detail, and with special regard
to the circumstances, to the peculiar difficulties, and also to the peculiar advantages
of our own day :—

> " I have lived long enough ; my May of life
> Is turned into the sere, the yellow leaf,"

said one who had misused that life. The
figure here employed is so clear as to call
for no explanation, and so solemn as to
need little comment. But it has a lighter
side,—one connected with the present
aspect of society,—its increased excita-
bility, and the increased need of wisdom
and of "*aplomb*" in its older members, if
they would not be crowded out in the
hurry and pressure of life nowadays.
From this point of view, which may not
be ignored, we shall pass on to another—

namely, the graceful, touching, and very close analogy which exists between the sere and yellow leaf in nature and that of metaphor. The thoughts it suggests may be very helpful, and by no means trite.

"Happiness," says Paley, "is a comparative term"; so is age—there is no defining it or its boundary line. We say of one acquaintance, "he never can have been young"; of another, "she never can grow old!" We congratulate our friends on being evergreens. Some of us are even unconscious of the process of ageing that is at work within—"grey hairs are on us here and there, but we know it not." A kindly light-hearted Irishman above eighty overheard some young men at his club eulogising him as a pleasant old fellow; he naïvely told a relative of this gratifying verdict, but added that the epithet *old* had rather surprised him; he must be allowed to think it somewhat premature.

Lady M., a vigorous old lady of ninety-six, informed a kinsman of the death of a common friend, aged eighty-eight, adding that poor Frances never had much constitution! Such vigour is rare indeed in one who has so nearly reached a century of years; happier, probably, are those whom growing infirmity, meekly accepted, reconciles to their approaching exit.

There was no lack of originality and playfulness in an aged gentlewoman, Mrs. Anna Maria A., resident about the year 1810 in the Yorkshire Wolds. Availing herself of a then very rare opportunity of obtaining a package from London, she wrote to a leading milliner for an assortment of caps suited to an old lady. The milliner in reply sent a selection of gay and juvenile head-dresses, with the information that there was no such thing as an "old lady" known in London. Mrs. Anna Maria bowed to the inevitable, and wore the head-gear, and told the story with much enjoyment.

This reminds me that a distinct barrier between middle life and old age has been swept away since the "taking of brevet rank" by elderly spinsters has become obsolete. The title "Miss" is at no time a graceful one ; even Flora MacIvor loses something of her dignity when styled by her French translator, "*cette charmante Miss*"; but the word becomes almost grotesque when applied to tottering eld. This incongruity is so much felt by many of our sisterhood, that one thinks a combined effort might be made to revive the respectable old custom with which the classical names of Mrs. Hannah More and Mrs. Frances Bowdler are associated.

The gray locks which, by some kind freak fashion no longer compels us to disguise under the masculine wig or feminine front, are no test of age—"*Poursuivants* of death" Shakespeare calls them ; and the poet of "Evangeline" describes in graceful Indian phrase her faded brow

C

as crowned with "death's blossoms"; but
these are figures of speech. Many a head
is streaked with silver while in its prime.
I know one of distinguished mien who,
at fifteen, was severely burnt; some years
later she reappeared in society restored
to health but with whitened hair and
colourless cheek. We all remember him

> " Whose hair turned white
> In a single night;"

and her, the Queen of France and of
sorrows, over whose gray discrowned head
but thirty-seven summers had passed
when she laid it on the block as on a
pillow of rest. A frequent guest of one of
our poets-laureate has often related to us
how in middle life the poet's head grew
grizzled; later on a constitutional apathy
and quiet stole over him, stilling the overworked brain, and the hair, which still
grew luxuriantly, after that resumed in a
measure the brown hue of early years.

Thus variable and, one may say, capricious are the advances towards the "sere and yellow leaf" of our bodily and mental condition. Though less capricious in its workings, the gradual change in nature from the living green of spring foliage to autumn brown is a vivid representation of human decay. I well remember how an eloquent "Gilchrist lecturer," on this subject, told us of the mysterious essence called chlorophyll pervading every leaf of every tree, and how, being acted upon by solar light, it produces both the intensely vigorous life and the dazzling green which amaze us spring after spring. Oh, the vigour of that life! See how the vine-tendril, drawn out to its utmost length, bounds back to its corkscrew position as soon as released. You have observed the .closely gummed-up leaf of the horse-chestnut, have you not? When a child I have more than once run a long darning-needle through it, and with wonder beheld

how after a while it has burst open, ex-
panding its five delicate fingers round the
cruel needle.   Is not this strong life
analogous with that of the little child?
Both are beyond our comprehension—God-
given and awe-inspiring.   I can never
forget the reverence and delight which
both inspired in the breast of Charles
Kingsley.   This attitude of his mind towards young nature and towards childhood we have often seen illustrated.
Walking one day with a friend through
a budding wood, a young tree in brighter
sheen than its fellows was pointed out to
him.   "Thank God for that!" he said
fervently.   One summer's day, which he
and his family spent in rambling with us
and botanising by the silver Dee, his
delight was to carry on his shoulder a
merry little maiden of two-and-a-half
years.   His strong-featured noble face, as
he turned it on the little one, recalled to
me by its rapt expression an old picture of

St. Christopher bearing the Divine Child through the waters.

The likeness between the summer wood in its glory and man at his best estate is patent to all ; but Hugh Macmillan points out a fact, less known perhaps, which bears on our subject. He says : " The sap in trees rises as profusely in autumn as in spring, but goes less to the leaves than to supplying the needful stores towards the development of fruits and seeds." Meanwhile chlorophyll, that elixir of life, disappears from the leaves, gradually carrying away the vital green; crystalline substances form within the cells of the autumn leaf, blocking all healthy action ; often tiny granules of starch choke its tissues, and so with little help from frost or wind it falls, not ungraciously pushed out of its place by next year's bud, but simply from decay of nature. So then each leaf hangs in its appointed place for its appointed time,

purifying the air by its healthful breath-
ings, and helping to screen bird and beast
and tired wayfarer from heat or rushing
rain ; and when it drops at last, it does
not become useless, but warms and fosters
those germs of vegetation which lie hid
in the breast of mother-earth.

Here is a parable for us, if we will take
it.   Are we in the way to grow old grace-
fully, usefully, calmly?   The elder men
and women in society, in the various
grades of life, in the cottage, farm, shop,
manor-house ; do they, as a rule, take
the lead their years entitle them to, and
raise the tone of those who see and mark
their daily conduct ?   Do they act so con-
sistently as to leave no doubt of their
purity of motive ?   As the rainbow in the
cloud unites fixedness and faultless truth
of outline with bright unearthly colouring;
do they, amid life's storm-clouds, exhibit
fixedness of principle softened by every
lovely and endearing virtue that can make

such principle winning? We have happy proof that many do this; many in public life or quiet homes show how far the little candle of individual worth can shed its light in a naughty world; many more are hidden from sight by pining sickness most bravely borne: such as these are the salt of the earth, and command respect from people whose aims are far lower, or who have no aims at all; but are they numerous enough to make themselves felt? "More fruit in age" is not very commonly the motto of elderly people; many seem to take it for granted that effort is no longer to be expected from them, that the time for ease and "*laisser aller*" is come, and so they sink into mediocrity and become cumberers of society, a weariness to themselves, and a trial to the good-nature of well-disposed young people.

Talleyrand once said that a failing may be worse than a crime; so it is often in youthful eyes. They are quick to note and to smile at any weakness which their elders betray, and on the habitual mediocrity we spoke of just now they have no mercy ; that one dead fly in the ointment makes it valueless.

Take an instance.   Edith, bright, clever, at fifteen a leading spirit in her High School, has come in, much imbued with a deeply interesting lecture on Milton, one of a series which Canon Barry has been delivering.   Grandmamma reclines in her easy-chair in the drawing-room ; on her knee is the third volume of the last novel, which the waning light has made her put down.   But the young eyes can still see, and Edith would fain read to grannie that lovely bit out of " Comus " on which the lecturer has just been commenting. May she?   " If you will, dear," replies grandmamma, languidly ; " but, on second thoughts, Mudie may send for this volume to-night, so, though it is a rather silly and improbable story, one may as well hear the end." Poor Edith! she ought to have known by this time that grandmamma seldom reads any intermediate book between her daily sermon and her afternoon novel. In our summary of the dangerous and evil instincts of the heart we gave precedence to that of indolence, mental and bodily, because it is so easily slipped into, and so deadening. In the case in point see how it reduced to a cypher one who might have been a loving household oracle in the home circle! Nevertheless, Edith's grandmother was a good woman; she would never willingly open a coarse or unprincipled work of fiction. Hers were not the lips from which I heard this sentiment: "Of course, So-and-so's books are not fit for my girls; but I read them all as they come out—they are so clever, and what harm can they do me at my age?" What harm indeed? as if we could ever be old enough to stain and sully our minds with reading coarse, flippant, or scandalous

works, however brilliantly amusing; as
though there were not abundance of graceful fictions, both in prose and verse, to
refresh the worn mind without feeding it
on such unwholesome stimulant or trash.
As the chameleon takes the hue of the
bough or rock it rests upon, so this profit-
less reading colours our conversation, to
the detriment of the dear young things
whom the King has straitly commanded
us not to offend or cause to stumble.

Look again. A man of distinction, as
far as appearance and manner go, carefully dressed in a style slightly too juvenile to suit the deep wrinkles and lack-
lustre eye that proclaim his seventy-five
winters,—this old man is kindly greeted
by a noble hostess, who allows him the
range of her palatial country - house.
Autumn after autumn he arrives as punctually as the swallows in spring, only,
unlike them, he does not punctually de-
part, for each year his round of visits

contracts ; people drop him, and take little trouble to conceal why. Here, however, the hostess, unselfish as true, acts on the motto, " Thy father's friend forsake not," in spite of playful remonstrance from her children. " Poor Sir John " is tolerated, and his daily visits to the kitchen and gastronomical suggestions to its *chef* are winked at. " Poor Sir John," see him with his hand up to his deaf ear vainly trying to catch the flying gossip at which others are smiling. " *Les mouches qui volent* " escape him now. Vainly he clears his throat to secure an audience for an anecdote of his own—his anecdotes are threadbare. ˙ Stay, he thinks he has that desired audience at last. The young people come about him, they make much of him, and by " fooling him to the top of his bent " succeed in extracting the history of an ancestor,—a " Sir John " who had been made a tool of, and then decapitated, by Henry VIII. I am afraid it was the subject of a small wager that this stock-story should be elicited ; I am afraid, too, that Sir John found this out, from a certain crestfallen piteous look on his weak old face. So here is an instance of " unregarded age in corners thrown," and submitting to be so thrown, rather than forego the gratification of vanity and self-indulgence, and live in manly independence in a modest and tranquil home.

PART III.

" I did dream of money-bags."—*Shakespeare.*

" Crabbed age and youth
Cannot live together."

Deterioration in age—Shown in a covetous spirit—
Illustration of this—Inadequate giving—" That wretched
guinea"—St. Paul's high standard in this matter—
" Working that we may have to give"—A fretful spirit—
Content and discontent—" Look on this picture and on
that."

HERE is yet another stumbling-block for advancing life taken from a lower step on the social platform. We find three patriarchal brothers, all somewhere about fourscore, dwelling together in a fine old manor-house, now a farm where their fathers dwelt before them. Nothing could be more rural or picturesque or neater than the place, with its huge bushes

of sweetwilliam and lavender, its rose-
mary - covered low walls, and its roof gay
with golden-green houseleek. Ranges of
bee-hives, fine poultry, and mild-eyed cows
with sweet breath, give repose and ani-
mation at once to the homestead. A
bold tor rising abruptly 200 feet forms
the background, and rich meadows slope
down to a broad estuary. The sober,
quiet, industrious old men, with their curly
white locks, thin pink cheeks and rustic
manners, look as primitive as their
surroundings ; and the finishing touch in
the direction of peacefulness seems to be
that for the last sixty years no woman
has dwelt under that roof-tree. But, alas,
as in Eden's bowers the tempter, " squat
like a toad at Eve's ear," made his evil
suggestion, so was it with these village
patriarchs. The disenchantment came
about thus : an accident, not serious, but
somewhat beyond the local surgical skill,
brought the eldest brother to his county

hospital for a while, where his quietness, simplicity, and civil-spoken ways, soon won all hearts. One day, however, his two brothers drove over, ostensibly to inquire after his health—really to claim a certain key which resided in his breast-pocket, and which fitted to two boxes at the farm, one containing his private store of *comestibles*, the other his hoarded money. His quota toward the household expenditure being wanted, the brothers begged for this key. He only hugged it the closer, grudgingly bidding them " if needs must " break open the provision-box, but on no account to meddle with the other. They insisted ; he resisted ; an unseemly squabble followed ; the sick man astounding nurses and patients by the dogged obstinacy he displayed ; until at last his baffled juniors drove away to their beautiful, but loveless abode.

We do not hoard our money like this old Oliver ; but we are much too apt to look upon it as absolutely our own, not as a trust and a branch of our stewardship. We fail to act on the principle clearly laid down while the world was yet young, that God, the Giver of all, claims a tithe of His gifts from us, for the use of His church and His poor. Hence the disgraceful fact that London hospitals are obliged to shut up wards, and refuse aid to suffering bread - winners; hence that "wretched guinea," as one from a London pulpit forcibly styled it — the stereotyped sum subscribed towards leading charities by men and women who deny themselves no luxury of yachting or Scottish moor, or pictorial or musical delight.

"Lazarus lies at thy door; thou knowest it not." One parting reflection on this subject I will venture, and it shall take somewhat of the form of a sum in Rule of Three. If the poorest working-man in St. Paul's day was not held excused from giving to his needy brother, "working with his hands that he may have to give to him that needeth," in what proportion ought the alms of the rich to be bestowed? Again, looking at those same inspired words, will a mere dole suffice, with no personal trouble taken, no effort of mind made? It can at least do us no harm to look this question in the face.

And now, a word to beginners in the race of life, concerning that defect, forbidding even in dimpled childhood, which often reappears on much the same lines in wrinkled age—I mean fretfulness. We, your seniors by fifty years or more, would bespeak much forbearance from you. By no effort of mind can you realise what it is to have drifted out of sight of youth, with its elastic joy and life ; out of sight of middle age, with its vigour and recognised usefulness. You cannot guess at the trial of dimmed eyes which will never more behold blue hills or sky, or the

" Lampeggiar dell' angelico riso "

D

on dear faces. The painful consciousness that only by a great strain can kind voices keep us *au courant* of passing events, is a trouble you cannot realise ; yet these things are, and they must at times bring sadness to the most cheerful members of the "sere and yellow" guild. To the sadness is often added some bitterness, where aims in life have failed. In your buoyant strength be merciful as you are strong. "Comfort the feeble - minded, support the weak." This kindness, dear young people, shall be made up to you a hundredfold, when, in your turn, the grass-hopper becomes a burden.

It has been our joy to have close relations with some who have wholly risen out of the foggy atmosphere of fret-fulness into the clear air of cheerful sympathies, fair love, and holy hope. To these we will gladly return later on.

Here are two very slight but true sketches from rural life, bearing on fret-

fulness and its opposite grace, sweet content.   Both lived in our retired parish,
and have slept among the rude forefathers
of the hamlet full half a century.   Jenny
had been, *par excellence*, the grumbler of
the village from her youth up, till all
power of recognising a blessing seemed
lost.   We almost dreaded our stated visits
to her specklessly clean cottage, some fresh
grievance being sure to crop up, and the
consoling psalm or chapter only eliciting
the morose remark that they made her
flesh go prickly!   The Squire has turned
his quiet cob down a muddy lane sooner
than encounter Jane, and the long-suffering
patience of our parson was tried to the
utmost, as the following sample will show:

"Good morning, Jane.   I'm glad to see
you looking a little better to-day."

"Better, sir?   Me better? when I be
tore to pieces wid the cough aw the night
through, hoosting and hoosting from th'
onder to the sunrise!"

The parson expressed his genuine sympathy. "I will get Dr. Cole to come this way, and bring something in his pocket to stop that cough. I wish it may. . . ."

"Kindly obliged to you, sir, but that be all one and the same as wishing me dead ; for the doctors, they do say, if my cough leaves me, I'm not long for this world."

The parson passed on, fairly silenced by this peevish soul. "He that followeth God grumbling," says Bishop Hall, "'tis all one as if he staid behind."

The parson had more comfort in our aged labourer, Daniel, long pensioned off, whom neither stiff limbs, nor deafness, nor rheumatic twinges could sour. A serene smile irradiated his thin face as he sat, crippled and ailing, in his chimney-nook through the long winter's day. Opposite to him sat his somewhat crabbed and unlovely old wife,—the object of much care and devotion on his part, and (if you will pardon the digression) a historical personage in our eyes. For had she not been snatched from the cradle and hid by her mother from Prince Charles Edward's Highlanders, when they marched through her native borough of Congleton in the '45 ? Molly always averred that she had had a narrow escape of being killed and likewise eaten by them savages. Well, on summer days Daniel would creep up to the Hall, besom in hand, to sweep up any stray leaves. I remember his last appearance. We children were then possessed with a mania for walking on tall stilts, and vied with each other in foolish and risky exploits. Daniel hovered round watching these doughty deeds with some solicitude, and memory retains the beautiful, benignant, and slightly regretful look on his face, as he softly said to me, " Missie, I wur nimble onst."

Thus trustfully, thankfully, with no repining, though possibly with a gentle sigh now and then, may each of us be found ready to pass from the warm precincts of life's active day to the cool restfulness of its twilight.

PART IV.

"Truth hath a quiet breast."

"Delight no less in truth than in life."—*Shakespeare.*

Deterioration in point of truth — Inaccurate thought leads to untruth—Instance of habitual exaggeration wrecking a life—Truth in work—Two Sunday-school teachers —Absolute truth in act not common—Unscrupulous dealings in middle life and in age—Instance, Dingle Brook— Deterioration in temper—Irritation—Anger—Self-control begun in youth—Discourtesy at home—The sarcasm— Example of William Wilberforce—Anger undignified— More fruit in age.

ONE of the strangest anomalies bound up in the heart of a little child is untruthfulness, sometimes verging on cunning. There is often no cause to account for it; and with the dawn of reason and under good training it dies wholly away. But the ill weed grows and strengthens where a feeble nature finds itself under the sway of a severe or hasty temper. There is nothing sadder than to see a timid little one cowering under the glance of an angry eye, and weakly trying to hide, or to shuffle upon another, the evidences of its wrong-doing ; and great is the guilt of the parent or nurse who, by manifesting more annoyance over a torn frock or a broken cup than over the lisped and faltering lie meant to hide it, lays the foundation of lifelong deceit.

The fearless child will sometimes romance in the most astonishing manner before he can speak plain. Probably, as a writer in the *Quarterly* says of the dog, the creature has a strong histrionic turn. See this sturdy little fellow of three rush into his mother's full drawing-room, in scant white drapery, shouting that his nursery is on fire. Mamma is sceptical on the subject; still, as she knows her nurse might be off duty at the moment, she dares not quite pooh-pooh the intelli-

gence. She rises—her friends rise also—
the infant actor has produced the sensa-
tion he aimed at, and retreats with gleeful
explosions of laughter to his cot. Johnnie
is happy in the possession of a wise mother
who will not suffer his exuberant fancy to
be a snare to him. But it was far otherwise with a clever, spirited, handsome
girl, whose career I shall briefly sketch.
Georgie was the only and motherless
daughter of a gallant naval officer—his
joy and pride. It is hardly too much to
say he worshipped the very ground she
trod upon. At sixteen she found herself,
with ill-trained mind and heart, and a
smattering of accomplishments, at the
head of her father's table whenever he
was ashore. Her quick repartees and
drolly-exaggerated stories passed for wit
with her father's guests; and if a few,
wiser and kinder than the rest, shook
their heads at her glaring departures from
truth, they were set down as " old fogies."

Early in her girlhood Georgie was left alone, for the father who had loved her, not wisely but too well, sank with his gallant ship and her crew under the salt sea-wave. She drooped for a while, then recovered her spring, and became the lively, sarcastic, untruthful Georgie of former days. She married early a quiet, gentlemanlike man in the army. Many years roll on and Georgie reappears, a hard loveless woman of sixty, her fine features sharpened, her voice harsh and reckless in tone. She has reduced her husband to a nonentity, and embroiled him with his family by mis-statements which did not err on the side of good-nature. Happily, one or two of her people-in-law were exceptionally kind, excusing her folly on the plea of the wretched bringing-up she had had. It would seem, if one might reverently say so, as if the plea had been allowed by Him, the Judge, strong and patient, whom we provoke every day. She was laid low at a watering-place on the south coast by a lingering and agonising disease, and there, under the guidance of a wise and earnest parish priest, the erring soul returned, we humbly believe, to its God. She became as a little child, humble, thankful, and true. One trait only will I mention, because such an impress of sincerity stamped it. When the doctors prescribed a daily anodyne to lull pain and give some hours' sleep, she steadily declined it. "No," she replied; "I have wasted my years, and the time for repentance is short; let me keep my senses clear for prayer to my God, if so be He will listen to so great a sinner."

What says the poet Calderon?

> "Heaven holds not so many stars,
> Nor the sunbeams so many motes,
> Nor the sea so many waves,
> Nor the fire so many sparks,
> As He hath mercies and forgivenesses."

The corner-stone of education must be truth. Dr. Johnson's aphorism, " If a child should say a thing happened in *this* window, whereas it happened in *that*, fail not to set him right," may appear strait-laced, but is wise.[1] Vagueness is the parent of untruth. The bringing-up of boys, and their course of study, has a tendency to produce accuracy ; but, as a rule, the education of girls, till very recently, has not been calculated to strengthen their reasoning or reflecting powers. " Women are so hopelessly illogical," said a clever man thirty years ago, with a shrug of good-humoured despair, "that it is waste of time to demonstrate anything to them." The feminine mind must revolve round something, and unless that something be truth, acted out in candour, rectitude, and

[1] Verbal accuracy may be carried too far, as when the professor of astronomy refused in common parlance to use the words " sunrise " and " sunset "; or, as when the little maid of all work, when asked whether the kettle boiled, answered, " No, sir, but the water do."

a "conscience as the noonday clear," self
will become the fatal centre of her being.
Hence the desire to shine, to be con-
spicuous at any cost, and what more silly
or more dangerous? Affectations of all
sorts come of it—slang, *outré* dress, de-
vices both in apparel and furniture falsely
called æsthetic, but a pain to the true
artist-eye, ornament, justly called "the
relief of substance," so overloading it that
the satiated taste all but "pines after
ugliness," so it be plain and solid.

Since it is obvious that youth should
be the training for middle life, and middle
life for age, is it not all-important that
we should set out with a true standard,
honestly trying ourselves by it as we go
along? Mark those two girls teaching
their Sunday classes side by side. Mary,
true of heart, has, as usual, carefully prepared the lesson at home ; so, though the
room is rather close, and the children
fidget at first, and her head does ache a

little, yet her cheerful earnestness proves catching ; they hang on her clear words, and by and by go away with some increase of happy Bible knowledge, some verse or collect that will come to their aid in future time of temptation. There is a true link between these little souls and hers. Not so with Selina ; she supposes it is expected of her to take a class, so she goes, not very often, nor very punctually, and she trusts to the inspiration of the moment as to what to say to the "little wretches." Feeling no interest, she kindles none ; collect or hymn is droned over, with no insight into its meaning, and it is a relief to both parties when the rector looks in to dissolve the assembly.   Is Selina's true work ?

The same test applies to work amongst the poor and sick, which often degenerates into a hurried running in and out of cottages with no particular aim.   Selina looks in on bedridden old Becca, who would so like "a chapter" to cheer her loneliness; for her sister is out charring all day, and when she does come in, stiff and tired, she is "as glum as a mourning-coach." Selina is really sorry for Becca, and would fain stay, but she sees a hand, the minute-hand of her little French watch, that beckons her away to a garden party, so she takes her leave, vaguely promising to come again. Becca sighs, and mutters to herself that she would be badly off indeed if Miss Mary were not "on a different pattern; *she* wur true as steel!" Yes, "true," that is the cardinal virtue of life; and do not imagine that Mary enjoys a garden party, or a ride to the meet with the Squire her father, less than other girls; she has a fresh and keen power of enjoyment, and one reason for this may be that amusement is, with her, subordinate to daily serious occupation. If duty and amusement clash, amusement goes to the wall, quietly and without a word, though possibly not without a sigh. "*Fais ce que dois, advienne que pourra*" is the only principle on which work can be done, to which the old may look back with thankful comfort. This applies, of course, to man and woman alike, to none more than our young clergy, whose perseverance in solid self-denying effort is sorely tried nowadays by the round of innocent little dissipations pressed upon them by the laity, sometimes from pure kindness, sometimes from an unacknowledged wish to make their presence a sanction for frivolity, and, in fact, to bring down their spiritual pastors to their own low level. Where this endeavour succeeds many a poor Becca is the loser by it; but the pastor himself is the greatest loser.

It may be that such reflections hardly come within the scope of this "my so littel boke," yet the fact is forced upon thinking people that, in haunts of business as well as in society, absolute truth of word and deed is not very common ; men will act the lie they might hesitate to speak ; and, saddest of all, the older they grow the more callous and unscrupulous do they become.   We not seldom see heads of firms authorising or winking at such practices in their establishments, that it is a miracle if any of their clerks come out with clean hands.[1]   How many a committee has its "Mr. By-ends," and its "Mr. Facing-both-ways"!   Some that I know have laughed at Pope's axiom, "An honest man's the noblest work of God," supposing honesty to be an every-day and even humdrum quality ; "are we not all — all honourable men and women ?"   Would indeed that it were so, and that we could claim that glorious

---

[1] A paper read by Mr. Skey, of Tamworth, at the Church Congress at Stoke-on-Trent in 1875, throws much light on this subject.

title, " The righteous nation that keepeth
the truth " !   But we fall far short of this,
and " All men seek their own " would be
nearer the mark in describing English
society now.   We must watch over the
generous and sanguine spirit of youth,
lest a sudden and rude awakening to
this fact should do them moral harm.

An opulent resident of great influence
in the borough of N—— is chairman of
a committee, which has at this moment
a desirable annuity in its gift.   There are
several candidates—one, a striving and
needy widow, has been at the top of the
list for six years, and has by far the
strongest claim ; but this gentleman has
an old dependent, recently invalided, for
whom some provision must be made, so
he spares to take of his own cash, and
by means of a little contrivance and con-
nivance obtains the pension for her.
What is it to him that the poor widow
turns away with meekly-folded hands, and

goes back to her garret for possibly six years more of penury and hope deferred? Look at that busy and energetic town-councillor, an habitual speaker in favour of "total abstinence"; yet, for fully ten days before the last election, it is an open secret that he set all the taps in his ward flowing gratis, with what results of sin and shame I leave you to guess. Is there not a lie in his right hand?

"Such things are of daily occurrence," was the grave reply of a business man well known in the City, to whom we *made our moan* on these departures from truth in act.

We only sketch such portraits lightly, and with the practical end of rousing ourselves and others to work on the side of truth and light against the active enemies of both. We cannot take up a newspaper without finding startling evidence of their activity. Already the ground beneath our feet rings hollow, warning us that our prosperity, if not built upon a strong foundation of truth and honesty, is sure to crumble and to fall.

When but eleven years old my faith in, and reverence for, age received a severe shock, as you shall hear. It was a wet gloomy evening in September, more than fifty years ago, in the dark ages when railways were not. It is hard now to recall that time when no trains thundered, nor telegrams flashed past our quiet gates which opened on the king's highway betwixt London and Liverpool. But that road was by no means dull, for many stage-coaches in their trim yet picturesque array went by. Tantivy, Red Rover, Hirondelle, and many more had their appointed times ; and then with twanging horn, splendidly horsed and appointed, passed His Majesty's mail. On summer nights when windows were open, and no sound but the barn-owl's cry or sedge-warbler's song broke the stillness — if, perchance, one lay awake, the night mail from London might be heard smoothly and rapidly rolling on, till lost in far distance. But on this particular night nothing was to be heard but the ceaseless pattering of rain on the full, though faded, foliage of our wood. At sunset only had there been a momentary break and lifting of the clouds ; then a tall dark column of vapour had stood out against a pale sky, its top lost in the general blackness, its base resting on the Derbyshire hills. We slept, as only youth can sleep, through the hurly-burly, and woke to newly-swept and garnished skies. But with morning light came terrible tidings confusedly told. That waterspout over the Derbyshire hills had deluged the channel of a brook which had heretofore flowed tranquilly through moorland and meadow into our neigh-bourhood. About a mile off it ran along a narrow valley lying east and west, and passed under the highway, which was crossed by a not very solid temporary bridge. Here the road from the south came down a steep declivity to the bridge. It appears that about midnight the swollen waters suddenly poured into the vale, turning it into a lakelet, and, rushing and crowding under the narrow archway of the bridge, they swept it clean away. Immediately after this crash the mail from London arrived at a quick pace; the night was dark as pitch, and the light of the lamps dimmed with rain. The coachman, guessing nothing of that chasm before him, whipped up his team for the opposite hill; in a moment his vehicle floundered and sank in the turbid stream. There were two inside passengers, both gentlemen, said our informant. One had been drowned in the coach, the other was still missing. There were several outside travellers, two of them, if I remember right, women. It would have gone badly with them had not the driving-seat been

shared by a young naval officer, who had
all his wits about him, and one by one
helped or dragged them from their pre-
carious hold on bushes and brambles to
the firm bank.   Imagine our grief and
dismay at this intelligence, and our excitement when the lady, who had charge of
us in our parents' absence, announced her
intention of repairing to Dingle Brook at
once, taking us with her.   This last
proposition, however ill-judged, was well-
meant, for the lady held peculiar and
gloomy religious tenets, which made all
mirth and laughter sinful in her eyes.
We were rather given to transgress in
this particular; so, acting on the proverb,
" High spirits is the mother of foolishness," she carried us off to Dingle Brook.
The early sun peeped over the shoulder
of the south-eastern hill into that green
hollow, and was reflected by a thousand
raindrops on the crimson and yellow
leafage of the bramble thicket.   The

stream had returned within its banks, leaving a layer of mud on the adjacent fields. There on its side lay the royal mail, its lining torn to shreds ; there lay a drowned horse ; workmen were "fettling" the broken bridge ; others were dragging for the missing passenger, whose body was shortly afterwards recovered. The rescued travellers were all gone, having been dried and fed at a farmhouse hard by. The gallant sailor had hastened away at peep of dawn to a town sixteen miles off, where his young bride was awaiting him, for it was their wedding-day. She might well be proud of him, for he had crowned his brave deeds that fateful night by scrambling up the steep northern hill just in time to arrest a Liverpool coach which was blindly rushing into the chasm. If he yet lives, how happy must the recollection make him !

With bated breath and beating hearts we followed Dame Deane into her thatched cot, and there, with the light from the diamond-paned window full on his still white face, lay the dead man. No trace of struggle now—all calm repose. I have seen marble effigies since, that brought him to mind. The broad brow, the closed eyes, the unusual length and breadth of the frame, the soft scanty gray hair just stirred by an air that crept in under the lattice. His hands were hidden beneath the sheet. My blood seemed to freeze as I stood looking, silently, intently, not without a vague sense of the beauty and grandeur of death. Miss Thanet called us away, and we walked home in as sad and sober a mood as even she could desire.

That day's mail brought from the south certain officers of justice in hot pursuit of a gentleman well - known and hitherto much respected in the philanthropic world. For years he had been the trusted treasurer of more than one charity. Only three

days before had it transpired that the
miserable man had defrauded those insti-
tutions of several thousands, and taken
his passage under an assumed name from
Liverpool to New York. The officers
were, as I said, in pursuit of this man ;
they found him, or rather they found his
mortal part, in Dame Deane's cottage.

"There are no tricks in plain and
simple truth," therefore do we hold it
so dear. So much indeed do our feelings,
if not perverted, recoil from deceit, that it
is a relief to turn from it to the last count
in our indictment—anger, ill-temper, viol-
ence of spirit. It is like exchanging the
mephitic vapour of a closed cavern for
outward air, pure, though charged with
electric matter. In the nursery-world we
would rather witness the quick passionate
slap dealt by one baby hand than detect
the sly pinch administered by another.
In advancing life what so hateful as the
"snake in the grass"? Openness con-

dones a good deal of unpleasant and unjust dealing, and makes forgiveness easy and a return to the *entente cordiale* possible. So far so good; it is well to be lenient towards infirmity of temper in others, remembering how much indulgence our own faults need. Moreover, what know we of their physical condition of heart or brain, their past training, their inherited weaknesses? Only, while we show indulgence towards the wrong-doer, we must not make light of the wrongdoing; we cannot cleave to that which is good unless we also *abhor* (mark the word) that which is evil.

Then, again, we must be as strict towards ourselves as we are tender of others; this is not quite the usual practice. That passionate old man, whose language under provocation is far from select, says complacently, "There is no malice in me, a little bluster, that is all." We have all heard, possibly uttered, such

words as these : " Well, I do plead guilty
to quick strong feelings, and they need a
safety-valve sometimes," etc. etc.   Some
of us are apt to speak of our sensitive-
ness thus, not without some self-com-
placency, applying a pretty word to a
very ugly thing—in plain English, ill-
temper.   Now, unfortunately, the most
ungoverned spirits generally get most of
their own way ; it is conceded to them
for a quiet life ; and so the remark of a
certain shrewd old Scotchwoman comes
true : " My bairn, mark me, 'tis not the
cleverest nor the wisest head that rules
the hoose, but just the warst temper."
The love of power, thus gratified, grows
by what it feeds on, and a turbid, selfish,
unamiable, decline of life is the result.

As this is not a treatise on education,
one homely remark of an old nurse will
comprise all I need say as to the treat-
ment of a passionate child : " I never yet
laid a finger on nursling of mine while he

was in the hot fit of his anger, neither did
I speak a sharp word.   I would just pop
him under the bedclothes to unbethink
himself, and I would take my knitting
and sit near him, and by and by a little
sobbing voice would come off the pillow,
'Kiss me, nursie, I'm sorry'; and my darling would be mild as milk after that."

In theory we all know that only by
prayer and watchfulness can the evil spirit of
anger be cast out ; and I believe that many
a blithe schoolboy, many a merry-hearted
maiden, knows it practically ; though, with
the reserve about holy things which char-
acterises youth, they could not lay bare
their thoughts even to the tenderest
mother.   Nor would the wise mother
wish it ; enough for her to watch the
dawning gleam of self-control, the spark
of sudden anger quenched without a word,
and only to be guessed at by the flushed
cheek and kindling eye ; enough for her
to rest assured that her boy, her girl,

knows the bliss of self-conquest through Him who, by the freest of free grace, claimed that boy, that girl, for His own soldier and servant, in holy Baptism.

It is the multitude of untamed or half-tamed souls, that have never heartily taken up this service, which makes our world the quarrelsome unquiet place it is, which sows strifes and jars in every neighbourhood, and what Mrs. Gaskell calls "miffs, tiffs, and cold shoulders," even in the guarded sanctuary of home. "If one may not be rude to one's nearest relations, who may one be rude to?" asked a chivalrous school-boy jestingly; but in some homes the sentiment seems acted upon in good earnest. Snapping, that odious form of treason against good manners, becomes a habit with old and young; you are ashamed for them, but they are not ashamed for themselves. From this comfortless state of things it is no hard matter to come to the angry accusation, the sharp retort, or,

worst of all, because the arrow is tipped
with poison, the sneer. Let me just say
that the sneer is the form in which old
people of ungenial and testy humour most
often annoy and perplex their juniors,
putting a strain on the sweetest tempers,
and souring less sunny natures. Where-
fore, if you would not play the part of an
east wind on green shoots, refrain from
any but the most gentle sarcasm.

Take a lesson from the great William
Wilberforce. It was a strict rule with
him to keep within its sheath the polished
weapon of satire of which he was a
master. One night, however, he broke
his rule, under immense provocation. His
devout turn of mind, though tempered by
playfulness, exposed him to more obloquy
than we dream of now; so it happened
that a young M.P. accused him, in a
heavy but flippant speech, of being *religi-
ously facetious!* Mr. Wilberforce, thrown
off his guard, fired up, and, amid loud

cheering, observed that the honourable member had proved to the House that there was such a thing as being *irreligiously dull!* But when some friends afterwards complimented him on this happy retort, he expressed unaffected sorrow for having indulged in sarcasm at the expense of that charity which suffereth long and is kind.

It must be confessed that uncontrolled anger does not wear a dignified aspect when, for example, exhibited by men of ripe years or high position. Our own King John rolling on the ground and biting at straws when vexed; Napoleon I., at St. Helena, seizing his gun in a rage and popping at the cocks and hens which one day trespassed into his shrubbery. These cut but sorry figures; nor does the great Czar of Babylon command our respect when, " full of fury," and the form of his visage changed by it, he consigns the three children, blameless and grandly faithful, to the furnace. We might not be far wrong in designating King Ahab as "a poor creature," when in angry disappointment he lies on his bed and turns his face to the wall, to muse helplessly on Naboth's honest refusal to sell his property. Such a state of mind only needed the suggestions of an artful woman to ripen into crime.

To return to our own day. What have elderly people to do with litigation, when they ought to be perfecting their peace with God and man? Yet, how many wantonly throw themselves into lawsuits, which by no stretch of the epithet can be called "amicable." Again, what a preparation for her near exit is that of the "*femme terrible*" who quarrels with her good Rector for some little discrepancy of opinion on some point on which he probably knows best, thwarts him at every turn, and orders her tenants away from their parish church?

F

These are true pictures, from which we turn gladly to portraits of another complexion—life-sketches of some who followed with undivided heart all that is true, lovely, and of good report, bringing forth more fruit in their age, not less, as the manner of some is.

PART V.

" The soul's dark cottage, batter'd and decayed,
　Lets in new light, thro' chinks which time has made."
　　　　　　　　　　　　　　Waller.

Life a probation in small acts as well as in great—Growth requisite in loving, loyal, reverent obedience—Lady B.'s counsels as to usefulness in later life—If age is to command respect we must not be ashamed of it—New problems in society—Young brains overtasked—Need wise soothing or bracing—Rush Londonwards—Amazing freedom accorded to young people—Traceable in part to steam—In rapid travelling—In increased manufactures—In printing—Reading often superficial and exciting—Excitement in charitable works—In religious services.

"THE heart of childhood is all mirth," says the special poet of childhood. But well he knows, and many lines in his most melodious *Lyra Innocentium* help us to know, that beneath the joyous sunlit bubbles of mirth are strong springs mixed with much evil sediment. The effects of this in after-life we have tried to sketch. Now let us recapitulate those better instincts which, we humbly believe, were in the thoughts of our blessed Lord when He took that little child to Himself, and bade His disciples take pattern by him. They are—love shown in acts of faith and loyalty and growing obedience, repentance for wrong done, forgiveness of wrong received, self-forgetting generosity, patience that crowns all. If, through life-long practice in a strength not our own, these things be in us and abound, we might be a tree of health to those who grow up under our shadow. Now as to loving service, we are too apt to think it can only show itself in distinct acts and on great occasions, whereas, it rather consists of a frame of mind in which every power we possess—common-sense, tact, playfulness, quick wit,—all are pressed into that service. Nothing is counted too small to be carefully and well done ; for is it not part of the offering that is daily going up to the Master ?   And do not little things on little wings bear little souls to heaven ?   We do not scorn the crumpled nosegay shyly offered by our infant Sunday scholar—the best it has to give.   The pleasure with which we receive those double daisies or buttercups may read us a hopeful parable as to the acceptance of our own worthless gifts.   Such a habit of mind goes far towards keeping it young, and consequently in sympathy with the young, and that is a great point gained. Now let us go into some details, small but not trivial, since they involve the question of faithfulness.

"Do not," said one of the wisest and best, as well as most beautiful, of women, to me forty years ago—"do not, like too many, allow indolence or self-pleasing in trifles to creep over you when youth wanes ; keep up a restful—not restless— activity ; don't let a shower or an east

wind keep you indoors—properly clad
and shod they will do you no harm ; and
your friends will be able to reckon on
your good offices when they need them.
Look intelligently to your poultry-yard,
your garden, your household ; never
through idleness suffer the control of this
last to slip out of your fingers, thereby
turning, as too often happens, faithful
servants into exacting masters ! These
homely duties promote strength and cheer-
fulness. Thus the healthful body and
healthful mind will enable you to bring
the experience of a long life to the benefit
of those about you, just when they have
become most valuable." I believe Lady
B. has saved not a few from becoming
hipped, useless, and discontented, by counsels like these. Unlike the writer who
published rules for composing good plays,
and showed what was a bad one by his
own, she fully lived up to her standard.
She used to quote the quaint advice of

an old retainer in her family : " Learn all you can ; you will never walk the heavier for what you know."

Secondly, and briefly, for the subject may be trite to some, if we wish our age to be respected, we must not be ashamed of it ourselves. As the delightful country parson touchingly says, "a certain sadness at leaving the prime of life behind for ever is part of our nature, and not in itself wrong." Those who by choice or otherwise have never married, and so leave none to perpetuate their name, feel this touch of nature most ; but, God be thanked, grace has a remedy for this as for every human craving. Only let our hearts be fixed where they ought to be, and all things fall into their proper place at once ; our life may be a struggle but can never be a blank. He who has told us plainly that He will not accept the second place in any heart knows how to satisfy the heart. That unique and divine link with Him gives also a value, a depth, an unearthly hope, to our ties of home and our friendships ; we feel they are but in their germ here ; He hath provided some better thing for us, in which sure trust we go on our way rejoicing. Thus regarded, age is an honourable state, not one to be ashamed of. It is the affectation of youth in dress or manner that makes us ridiculous, and gives a just handle to our young critics. Miss Edgeworth tells us of two ladies whose struggle for precedence was quelled by one of the company suggesting that the elder of the two should walk out first. Both vehemently declined precedence on that ground. Can anything be more pitiable than this ? We knew a certain pleasant admiral who used to test the for-titude of maiden ladies by recalling with merciless accuracy the exact day, month, and year, in which they danced with him —their first dance at their first ball. Most of them bore the ordeal, albeit a some-what public one, with smiling philosophy.

Though historians tell us that sumptuary laws are a proof of weakness in a government; yet in our sere and yellow guild it must be said that scrupulous neatness, quiet good taste, and, where the means are ample, a certain richness of dress, beseems its members.   It is one of the "*petites vertus*" St. Louis loved, thus to please and satisfy young eyes, and such a harmony between the faded person and the apparel will not appeal in vain to their innate sense of fitness.

After all, how could any of us seriously wish to clip the wings of time in our own case, unless we could do as much for our life's companions?   We could not stand still if we would, and surely, we would not if we could!   Is it not much happier to journey onward, as the old, old pilgrim song in the Vosges mountains words it—

"Un à un
Par le chemin—des saints,
Deuxadeux—vers les cieux"?

Our third subject of thought is more complex ; it is the spirit in which loving loyalty and obedience should lead us to regard the quickly changing aspects of society.

"The world is in its dotage," said Goldsmith's charlatan to Moses Primrose, and Moses Primrose implicitly believed him. Some such impression flits across the mind, as from our loophole of retreat we gaze out on the great Babel anxiously —very anxiously, for many young souls are there in whose life our life is bound up. The outlook is rather a wild one— professions overstocked, and only entered upon by such a strain of brain-work as many young heads cannot bear. This applies to all grades, from the pale pinched pupil-teacher upwards. Many a manly honest young fellow, not devoid of mother-wit and observation, is thrown back because outstripped by others inferior in worth and in common sense. Is this mushroom growth of the last forty years altogether wise? However this may be, it certainly gives abundant scope for happy and healing relations between elder people and the struggling young aspirants on the threshold of life. They are particularly open to sympathy, so it be well-timed, not loquacious nor fussy. Some of us may be able to help them in their work ; or we may help them to unbend from it ; we may playfully check the "cocky;" or we may brace the overstrung candidate for honours by instilling the spirit of those grand lines :—

> " 'Tis not in mortals to command success,
> But we'll do more, Sempronius, we'll deserve it."

Thus, though the starch granules may be thickening in our wasted tissues, the remembrance of our spring, when those tissues quivered with the light and life of chlorophyll, will keep us free from selfish nonchalance.

Observe this lady of fourscore and five

with pallid but animated features, and eyes undimmed and full of intelligence ; she sits before her chess-table, serenely but intently watching for her antagonist's next move. He is a good player, but then so is she; and the frequent afternoon game of chess with him or with others serves as a grindstone to sharpen the intellect without in the least sharpening her temper. He muses, hesitates, plays ! She surveys each remaining piece on the board rapidly yet thoughtfully ; then, with an arch kind smile which disarms the fatal word of its sting, says Checkmate ! Can you be surprised that keen young wits or overworked elder ones alike consider it a privilege to enter the lists with our honoured friend ?

Another change in modern life is the marked diminution of country hospitality. Forty years ago there was a good deal of pleasant and genuine intercourse carried on in our country houses, and many a bright and highly-connected girl was per-

fectly satisfied with these informal gather-
ings and gaieties at her own and other
country homes. " *Mais nous avons changé
tout cela.*" The general complaint is that
in the country there is *no neighbourhood.*
What are called bad times may partly
account for this really unfortunate state of
things ; but there seems a yet deeper
reason. People now economise and shut
their doors for ten months in the year that
they may have funds for two months'
London season ; that they may present
their daughters, give an entertainment or
two, peradventure a ball ; for which some
London *habituée* will provide the guests,
and by dint of coercion and great agitation
may get asked by leaders of fashion in
return. They count themselves happy if
they obtain a certain number of greetings
where no kindness is, and are present
at the last musical or dramatic novelties.
I believe the old plan for people of
limited income of going up quietly for a

fortnight or so of real enjoyment of art,
pictures, etc., answered better than to-day's
more ambitious doings ; certainly it argued
more self-respect in English matrons. We
cannot on £2000 a year attempt with
impunity what people can do on £5000
a year. Something must be foregone if
we would pay our way—a self-evident
proposition which, however, some of us
are slow to face. But face it we must ;
and could we use any influence we possess
better than in persuading our young
people at home, at school, at college, or
in society, to flee from debt and from
such reckless expenditure as entails it, as
from a scorpion ?

There is another glaring change which,
I confess, almost tempts me to transgress
Solomon's injunction, " Say not the former
days were better than these !"—it is the
amazing freedom of action and thought
now enjoyed by our rising generation. It
is no part of our scheme to account for

this phenomenon, though I suppose if we wished to do so with that brevity which is the "soul of wit," the one word *steam* would not be far from the mark. Its results are magical: the girl who used to wait for some uncle or guardsman-brother to escort her by mail-coach to town, sleeping one or two nights on the road, is now put into her train, committed to the guard and to her own native good sense and dignity, and in ten or twelve hours wafted to her destination. No longer need careful fathers take turns to fetch their own and each others' boys from school. We remember what our good neighbour Mr. L. had to endure on one such occasion, when the three youngsters in his charge strenuously attempted to play at leap-frog in the post-chaise. Those days are over! "If a cross wind do blow," says a chronicler in Edward IV.'s reign, "it shall take a man thirty days to sail, with much tacking, fro' Bristol to

Calais." Now, be the wind fair or foul, not men only but tender and delicate women, amid much luxury and small hardship, find themselves at the Antipodes in five weeks, or at Calcutta in three. When the world can be thus easily girdled, who will stay at home? Only the old, who must perforce do so. Thus, young travellers are much thrown on their own right feeling in very mixed society. "Forewarned is forearmed"; and the tender warning from revered lips may save from many a false position.

The power of steam which so increases our mining and manufacturing population has its drawbacks and its dangers. Even boys and girls may earn good wages. Many of them bring all to the wise provident mother gladly, even begging as a favour leave to take back a trifle for some good periodical or harmless amusement. But many more, as I have sorrowfully witnessed, make these earnings a handle for license ; threatening to break away from home and lodge elsewhere, unless late hours and Sundays profaned are altogether winked at.   This wretched abuse is almost beyond cure, but it is not beyond prevention, as you may see in localities where squire or parson or mill-owners' families take the trouble to provide safe resorts and safe amusements in or out of doors for the young " hands."   Where they show their personal interest by mixing at stated times with these young people the good results are doubled.   If you have not seen it, you would be surprised to observe what a charm the gentle voice and smile of an aged superior can exert on the veriest lout ; it may be the saving of such an one to be thus individually cared for.

Steam adds enormously to the amount of printed matter in the world.   The prophet Daniel, in his closing chapter, utters very remarkable words by no means alien to this subject : " Many shall run to and fro, and knowledge shall be increased." His first clause reminds us of the growing restlessness we have alluded to ; his second might apply in part to the rapid printing which spreads alike good and evil knowledge. Books, periodicals, reviews, newspapers ! Life is too short for the demands they make on each day ! The *Times*, we are told, prints daily as much matter as is contained in a three-volume novel ; in its pages we study our modern history, or, at least, the events that will crystallise into history. With what feverish eagerness have we looked for it at critical times, when the passion-waves of war or politics have " fiercely beat and mounted high " ! Other papers and pamphlets on subjects of the day have to be read ; but they must be read with care not to adopt every brilliant new theory propounded, or discard every sober-suited old maxim rejected by the ephemeral writer. Even religious

papers must be read with some reserva-
tion, as, however excellent in themselves,
they are bound by their very nature to
admit many articles and much correspon-
dence strongly tinctured with party spirit;
and, depend upon it, party spirit is an
almost unmixed evil. Convictions, deep
and strong, we are bound to have ; in all
subjects of practical importance we may
take a side—nay, we are bound to do so,
for what says the Persian proverb (?)—
" Egg is good and chicken is good, but
that which is between the two is only fit
to be thrown away." But we must hold
our opinions—say rather our principles—
with the least possible personal feeling.
It will save much disappointment and
many mistakes to be careful on this head ;
for few have attached themselves blindly
to a leader either in church or state without having cause to rue it.

To come to more solid studies. It
might be as well to point out to our

juniors that some modern histories are one-sided in their tone, and disguise under a vividness of colouring, akin to romance, very false and misleading outlines indeed. Those amongst them whose bias is to-wards democracy touch with somewhat ungracious contempt on the past; and yet there were giants in those days!

Is modern biography, that most inviting form of reading, always candid and trust-worthy? I read lately the record of a very holy and self-denying life devoted to God and His poor. One thread of human imperfection appears in the golden woof; it manifests itself in habitual disregard of counsel or remonstrance from those in authority, and in carrying on work by what they considered dangerously extreme methods. This form of self-will is por-trayed as pure heroism, and those who would have set bounds to it are accused, by no means fairly, of persecution—a charge difficult to repel, inasmuch as attack, if sharp and slashing, is more captivating to the unripe judgment than sober defence.   In this and other recent memoirs the fault seems partly to arise from their being published so shortly after the death of their subject that passions have not had time to cool nor party strifes to die out.   It is a pity that the unseemly hurry and bustle which mark our age should force their way into the tranquil kingdom of letters.

The spirit of change and progress makes itself felt in many of our novels, in which the self-made man, banker, doctor, solicitor, brewer, is almost invariably the hero, and clothed with a real interest. There is a true nobleness in the struggles and triumphs of such men which rouses and enchains the young ; and if we would keep our hearts in unison with theirs we, too, must recognise the greatness of self-help—not the surly self-help that toils and grinds on with no reference to a higher hand, but that which cheerfully works in conscious dependence on God.

" Progress and steam," says Mr. Nasmyth in his very interesting autobiography, "make the world less youthful and joyous !" Most true ; young people themselves are, as a rule, less young and joyous than their fathers and mothers were before them, for there is nothing so ageing as excitement; and where the fresh sweetness of a good home has not been known or not been appreciated, excitement is apt to mingle largely with the pursuit of pleasure, of art, of so-called charitable work, including public meetings, public speaking, bazaars, raffles, conversaziones, school or choir trips, even these last, not, as once, to some pleasant goal within easy reach, but fast and furious to some remote lake or city whence the party returns fagged and jaded at dead of night.

If the good in all this restless movement is to be developed, and the mischief

minimised, middle-aged people must not
shrink from their part in the guidance of
the social machine ; nay, more, they must
be ready, on occasions, to come to the
fore, and to remind our impetuous young
Jehus that the drag-chain has its uses as
well as the whip. Still, in all this, they
must speak hopefully. " Sow hope-
seed wherever you go," the great Bishop
Selwyn used to say : " we none of us
sow half hope-seed enough." I repeat
that parents, guardians, or sponsors, must
not shrink, if needful, from " coming to
the fore " ; nor need they, for in every
unperverted heart there resides an instinct
in favour of authority. It is a want of
knowledge of human nature that prompts
people to say, as they often do, " What
a happy footing that father and son, that
mother and daughter, are upon ; they might
be brothers, or they might be sisters !" But
such a footing between parent and child
—that of equality—was never intended ;

therefore it cannot be the best; neither is it lasting, for where filial respect is undermined, affection often becomes fitful and wavering, and not seldom you may see coolnesses, disobedience, and even unsanctioned marriages follow. Even short of such results home-love loses its delicate sweetness when respect is not a vital part of it; it rests with us both to inculcate and to deserve that respect.

Here is a case in point of a disorganised household: a respectable young person recently confirmed, and carefully prepared for Holy Communion, entered as maid into the service of a family in the same parish where she had been brought up. Week followed week and she never appeared among the communicants in her church, to the disappointment of her clergyman. Inquiry was made and the truth elicited: it was this;—her young lady was out late on Saturday nights, and had to be undressed in the small hours of Sunday morning. After snatching a few hours' rest she would rise and be dressed for early service at eight. On her return from this she again went to bed, not rising till mid-day, when the business of the toilet had to be resumed. Of course her maid could never attend morning church—it was not to be thought of. Does it not strike you that some guiding power is wanted here to save the young mistress from the risk of profaning holiest things, and to vindicate for the young servant her right to attend the heavenly feast, spread alike for rich and poor?

There is work to be done of the sad and solemn kind—that of gently leading back to God from paths of vice erring and fallen souls. Now, obviously, this is work fitted only for women of matured wisdom and love, directed by their clergy. How is it that when such come together to take counsel on the dark problems that encounter them, they are hampered at every turn by the presence of young girls who, with or without chaperons, have made their way to the meeting, urged manifestly rather by idle curiosity and love of the sensational than by any holier motive? Would not these young creatures have been far better at home? And might not their spare energies be trained by their mothers to works of cheerful kindness better fitted for their years? Nothing so blunts feeling and delicacy as such premature acquaintance with the depths of sin and misery.

Oh, the priceless blessing of good home-guidance amid the eccentric fashions of our day, saving those guarded ones from many absurdities—from extremes in dress and flightiness in talk, such as many in later life can never look back to without a blush! By the same means the more high-strung souls amongst them are preserved from the Scylla and Charybdis of Rome and Geneva, from placing human dogmas on an equality with divine truth, or from rejecting invaluable parts of that truth altogether.

PART VI.

" Religion—what treasure untold
Resides in that heavenly word."—*Cowper.*

Our aid needed by the young against the modern forms of unbelief—Flimsy in their nature—Insidious—Set forth in periodicals — In drawing-rooms, ball-rooms — By brilliant talkers—By women anxious to shine—Argument unadvisable—Scepticism paralysing—Reverence a safe-guard—Strength in gospel facts—In creeds—In Christian examples—Unbelief in great towns—Incident in London—Incident in Brittany.

THERE is, alas, a more subtle snare than those we have already named laid nowadays to catch unwary feet! This subtle snare is unbelief. A few words on its present shifting aspects, and on the best way of encountering or avoiding them, as may seem wisest, are all that come within our modest scope. The subject may not be altogether ignored, for so specious and so bold has unbelief shown itself of late that our affectionate care, and even our reasonings grounded on a thoughtful study of the danger, may be needed by those inexperienced ones whose confidence we possess. If by evil contact mischief has already been done, may not loving lips be privileged to suck the poison out of the arrow wound?

One danger of the present new phase of old unbelief is that men and women of sparkling conversation, and surprising variety if not depth of knowledge, carry it boldly into the heart of society, attract such listeners as are always eager for some new thing, and transform as many as they can into adherents. They beg the question as to our holy faith, dismissing it with an ease and levity which are hardly consistent with good sense or good taste. Instead of the ponderous tomes in which infidels formerly recorded their comfortless opinions, these for the most part embody their sentiments in pamphlets or periodicals, which, to our shame, lie on the table in many a so-called Christian house. In drawing-rooms, at dinner-tables, in the intervals of dancing, they see no incongruity in playing with topics which most of us hold sacred.

The teaching of these self-made " exiles from the eternal providences " is vague ; as when a " Positivist " bids us bring our being into absolute sympathy with universal humanity, but without stating how this process is to be begun or carried on. It is negative ; these writers, as a body, asserting that in our efforts towards perfecting our nature we need no recourse to supernatural aid—a Creator some of them allow us to feel blindly after, but Redemption in any form cannot be admitted. On this momentous subject they are not content to take their own line, and let us alone ; they wax aggressive, sparing neither insinuation, attack, nor sneer, against our happy faith.

Why this inveteracy it is hard to explain, unless on the principle that actuated the fabled king who, losing his right eye accidentally, took speedy measures to deprive all his subjects of theirs.

This ignoble eagerness to bring down others to their own level is happily not felt by all. Charles Kingsley has more than once told us of an infidel, known to him, who had his children instructed in Creed and Commandments, willing, he said, to "spare them his own wretchedness." One whom we cared for became the wife of a sceptic ; but he never spoke to her of his dark secret, never tampered with her religious convictions—nay, insisted on her carrying them into act by punctual church-going. What is commonly called " pride of intellect " had led this man astray ; but it was a three years' residence in Peru, amid a degraded society—priests and people alike corrupt and bigoted—which completed the ruin of his faith.

These unhappy men were, at least, free from the levity—the "*persiflage*"—which accompanies drawing-room discussion on the subject ; especially where vain women, anxious to shine, take a part in them. No one disliked this *persiflage* more utterly than Charles Kingsley. "Notwithstanding her opinions she is a charming little person ;" I heard a lady say to him respecting a young "Agnostic," whose contempt for Creed or Prayer was painfully apparent. "She is a charming little *fool*," he replied, with sad and sorrowful emphasis. That erring one died soon afterwards, and was laid, not in "God's Acre," but in a shrubbery planted with rose-bushes ; and labourers returning home after their day's work would make a *détour* to shun the place. I could describe from personal knowledge the abject terror shown by an unbelieving wife whose husband was suddenly called away by rapid illness.

"Of comfort let no man speak" at such

a moment where faith and hope are not, and love itself is all but drowned in selfish agony of fear. We would rather glance at the happier fate of a gentle girl misled for a brief space by the sophistries of one of those " leaders of thought," but led back by a tender father's reasonings and prayers to her Saviour's feet " in time to die His friend," as we humbly believe. Assuredly, looked at from the point of view of the dark valley, " the foolishness of God is wiser than men, and the weakness of God is stronger than men."

We have nothing to do here with argument, and especially on a subject so complicated ; but we may try to clear up our thoughts as to the causes of what I may term this phase of " drawing-room infidelity," and from what I am told by kind but keen observers, they seem to be mainly vanity, vacuity of mind, or that absorbing love of this present life, which makes many obstinately shut their eyes to any

outlook beyond it. " I have been thrown
with a good many Agnostics," says a
friend of mine, "mostly quite young people;
they are, in general, eager to press their
peculiar views upon one, but I always
decline arguing with them; reasoning
does not seem their forte, though some
of them have an amazing flow of talk;
they are curiously ignorant of the religion
which they affect to despise. I say
" affect," because there is a vein of affectation in the tone of these young talkers, a
modelling of their expressions on those of
their leaders, which often borders on cari-
cature, and betrays feebleness." This does
not remove danger; moths are feeble
creatures, yet undetected they may fret
substantial garments into holes. We will
guard our children from this; and as the
fresh young heart, like nature, abhors a
vacuum, we will exert ourselves to bring
within their reach bright, sensible, right-
minded young companions, whose com-

panionship may safely ripen into friendship. Thus guarded they will never crave for intimacy with those pitiable seceders from their cradle faith who may seek to mislead them.

Give them then good friends, good books, something definite to cling to. Our religion, thank God, does not rest on feelings, changeable as clouds, but on facts. The mystery of sin is a fact, balanced fearfully and wonderfully by the mystery of the Cross, also a fact, as completely proved as any in history. The risen Lord, the two blessed sacraments,— His gifts to us nearly 2000 years ago, so simple and unexciting in their outward form, so fraught with manifest grace for countless struggling souls,—the Old Testament with its exquisitely beautiful types and figures of redemption, and its prophecies providentially guarded by the Jews themselves, the beloved though blinded nation ; the glorious succession of God's heralds carrying to all ends of the earth the glad tidings that " the day-spring from on high hath visited us ;" all these are facts, telling facts, quite outside of ourselves ; they are safe guarantees for the spiritual and invisible parts of the divine revelation granted in infinite mercy to man. Let these realities be stamped on the soul, and then it shall still be strong even at those trying moments, incident to all, when the corruptible body presses down the spirit, and when flesh and heart fail.

" Do not dissipate your mind by reading too many human books on religion," said a very thoughtful and far-sighted bishop in my hearing ; " go at once to the well of Scripture undefiled, and make that your main study, helping yourself with the soundest commentaries ; let nothing dis-tract you from this."

In our day some young men, and not a few girls, are fond of introducing church

questions, discussions on the last remarkable sermon, and such-like grave topics,
into morning-visit or table-talk, but the
habit does not conduce to reverence ; and
so-called conversation on serious things, if
not carried on in a serious spirit, soon
becomes frivolous, and personal.   It is
quite another matter when, at fitting
moments, the elders take the lead, and
their juniors ingenuously and diffidently
follow that lead, "both hearing them, and
asking them questions."

Our minds are constituted somewhat
like those Indian cabinets, which most of
us have seen or possess.   Each subject of
thought that is worth retaining at all,
should have its own place in its own
drawer ; above all, our loyalty to faith
and religion, should be treasured in the
deepest, safest, strongest drawer,—I had
almost said the secret drawer,—not however to rust there ; far otherwise ; but to
be sacredly guarded and diligently used.

One glance at those wilder and fiercer forms of unbelief in the outer world, with which our juniors must inevitably have to cope. I suppose our hearts would sink, almost die within us, could we from our guarded nests guess at the ravages they make in the dark places—the courts, lanes, and cellars, of overcrowded London, and of every city in its degree; among the reckless men, the bold women, the unkempt wilful children, meant to be fair and sweet, but like flowers packed tightly into a vase, corrupting one another and the atmosphere around them. Can we wonder if at the tailor's shopboard, on the shoemaker's bench, in the mechanic's shed, "their talking is against the Most High;" and, in the prophet's words, they would be glad to persuade themselves, if the still small voice within would permit them, that "the Lord hath forsaken the earth"?

All this is very sad, very terrible, but not hopeless; a ray of light, unknown

before, has dawned on the darkness.
These 3000 London lay-helpers, who
meet annually under the dome of St.
Paul's, are the van of a noble army
coming to the help of the Lord against
the mighty. What wonderful powers of
organising, and of both doing and direct-
ing work of the most arduous kind, do
many of our town-clergy exhibit! The
very difficulties in their path seem an
attraction to these loyal-hearted men.
By dint of perseverance they get a hearing, and they get a footing too, among
" the masses; " and laymen will always be
found willing to help in wisely-planned
efforts, and to contribute that business
capacity which, rightly or wrongly, some
of our clergy are said to be deficient in.
Mission rooms, bright and hearty church
services and singing, addresses at the
men's dinner-time, powerfully written
leaflets, not scattered broadcast to be
trod under foot, but given with discrimi-

nation—all these, and the healing work of women who have learnt to obey as well as to command, must tell for good, and we must all help. The little child who saved up his pennies till he could offer eighteen to his vicar as the price of one tile for the chancel of the parish church, may read us a lesson, and so may a pair of very young twin-brothers, who denied themselves for a year their favourite luxury of sugar, that the proceeds might help their father, a hard-working clergyman, in some object he had much at heart.

There is a true and simply told narrative on the list of the S.P.C.K.'s valuable tracts called "If you rob me of my Bible, what will you give me in exchange for it?" I trust this tract will never be allowed to go out of print, for it is calculated to do, and has done, under my own eye, much good. A mechanic relates how, on a pleasure - trip with his family on the Thames, he is shocked by hearing a fellow-passenger on the steamer noisily declaiming against Christianity. No one attempts any reply, so, after a pause and a silent prayer, our friend speaks up gallantly and modestly in behalf of religion. His concluding words form the title of the tract. Some years later it was granted to him to see good fruit from that day's work. A workman, to whom I lent this narrative, returned it with these hearty words, "He's in the right of it ; there is a power o' fine books i' the world, but Bible's the masterpiece."

Some friends of a young officer gave me the details of a singular adventure which befell him some years ago in a rough part of East London, and as it bears on our subject you shall hear them. He was walking one evening along a low, ill lighted street, when the hum of voices and then a roar of applause drew his attention. Looking through a window into a large, low room, he saw it crammed

with men in their working - clothes, all
eagerly hanging on the words of an
orator at the farther end. The orator
was standing on a rather high platform,
and holding forth with much sound and
fury, though very insignificant in stature.
The officer, smitten with curiosity, made
his way into the crowded hall, and stood
almost unobserved among the " unwashed
artificers." His honest mind at once
recoiled from what he heard—bitter and
violent abuse of every Christian creed or
practice, and more especially of the great
truth that we are accountable for our
actions. This " wretched superstition "
of our being accountable for what we
do, the man specially inveighed against.
Fresh bursts of applause greeted these
sentiments. The officer could stand this
no longer. Working his way to the
farther end of the hall, he climbed up
the back of the platform, and took his
stand by the lecturer's side. Being tall

and strongly made, he presented a curious contrast to him in appearance. There was a pause of astonishment. "My friends," said the officer, "you have all heard what this gentleman says. He says we are not accountable for our actions. Very good. Then observe, my friends, I am not accountable for what I am about to do," and laying hold on the orator by the collar of his coat, he raised him from the floor and shook him two or three times energetically. Then setting him down, he repeated, " Now, mark me, I am not accountable for this act of mine — so the gentleman says." Peals of laughter greeted this performance from every side of the hall, then enthusiastic cheers for the officer, who bowed and went his way.

This is one way of destroying the prestige of a mischievous talker. It had, at least, the merit of success. Here is another :—

Between forty and fifty years ago a clergyman was presented to a small living in the north of England, and shortly afterwards asked by a neighbouring peer of infidel opinions to dine with him. He met at Lord ——'s table two or three brother clergymen, by no means of a high stamp, and was soon shocked and surprised at his host's scoffing remarks and profane witticisms. The guests remaining silent, Lord —— observed, "You gentlemen in black do not seem to enjoy the jest." "My lord," replied the new comer sternly, "there is one gentleman in black present, who enjoys it much." So saying, he left the house.

There is one form of acknowledging our belief in a present God and our sense of hourly dependence on Him, which appears to be rapidly falling into disuse in large dinner-parties—I mean saying grace before and after meals. Either the few words of lowly thanksgiving are miser-

of Truth.   Not, thank God, on our own merits shall we stand there, but on His who made "a full, perfect, and sufficient sacrifice, oblation, and satisfaction for the sins of the whole world."   I remember to this day, with a glow of comfort, the emphasis with which Dean Stanley, preaching in Westminster Abbey at a time when controversy ran high, gave in his adhesion to these words, which do indeed contain all our salvation and all our desire.   None the less, as proof of adoring thankfulness, does the Lord of Truth expect good fruit from us.   How can we best get this fruit to ripen under the shadow of the sere and yellow leaf?

First, then, as soon as we feel within ourselves a distinct lessening of strength and of vital energy, it would be well to begin transferring our work by degrees to younger shoulders.   If we are wise, we shall have prepared and trained the shoulders for it ; and, having devolved our work frankly and cheerfully, we must see that no jealousy, no hankering after lost power, no asperity if new methods are tried, and especially if they succeed, rankles within us. Many of us must have observed a sudden collapse of good and useful work, simply because the hand that guided it singly has been paralysed, and there is no one to take it up. The same thing holds good in family life. Surely every mother ought to admit her girls to some share in household management, or, at least, knowledge of it. For want of this how many pitiably ignorant young wives there are, whose dinners must contrast painfully in the husband's mind with the luxurious repasts his club has accustomed him to expect, and who, through sheer want of consideration, are capable of putting a guest into a damp bed ! So, like mercy, this graceful willingness to share, and in due season to resign, the reins of government is " twice blessed ;

small pittance of his own, and having in early youth registered a vow to try and advance God's glory in his birthplace, he had decided to remain there as a private individual. "This he has done," said one of his fellow-townsmen, "to our great comfort, and the present *curé* and he serve the church together in all peace and amity." Thus, passing rich with probably little more than £40 a year, the *vicaire* lived on. One of the good works he fostered was a day-school, where 200 needy children were taught, fed, and partly clothed by some kind sisters. On the day in question we revisited this school, warmly greeted by the sisters; we tasted the soup, inspected the cupboard full of coarse but clean garments, and listened to the quaint songs and versified sums of the little ones. Then the boys made their salaam, and 100 sallow, black-eyed small maidens in close calico caps curtsied their adieux and their thanks for our offering to their "*tronc des pauvres.*"   We passed thence into the cathedral hard by, with its deep shadows, its massive columns, and the delicate slender shafts of black marble creeping up them.   Some of us tried to sketch, and I remained alone watching the shifting effect of sunset light through some south-western windows, and then observing the solemn, almost oppressive gloom, that shrouded the eastern end. " Would these binocular glasses be of service to madame?" asked a deep voice at my side, that of the *vicaire* we afterwards ascertained.   An interesting conversation in low tones followed on the history of his beloved church, on its architecture and square chancel, making it probable that English masons had helped in the building.   "We have to thank your isle for greater things than these," he said ; "for did not saints from your Cornwall first preach the Gospel in

I

Brittany?" I ventured to point to a sprinkling of kneeling figures in the aisles, saying how much the beauty of column and tracery was enhanced by the living beauty of devout worshippers there. He sighed deeply. "Alas, madame, we have much cause to fear for our dear people," he said; "Paris is brought, as it were, to our gates by the 'iron road,' and floods of atheistical publications pour in upon us, destroying many. Do you see yonder altar? There, during the Reign of Terror, a Goddess of Reason was enthroned, and received the homage of a murderous rabble. Her grandchildren still live in this town; must we not fear that similar horrors may be enacted again?" I was much moved by his sad earnestness, and the too great likelihood that his fears might be realised. There was a pause, and then, with kindling eye, and a deep glow on his olive cheek, he added, "But what says our Lord? He says—and the words are recorded in your

version of Holy Scripture as in ours—
'The gates of hell shall not prevail.'"
Those were the *vicaire's* parting words;
and then, as John Bunyan says, he went
on his way, and I saw him no more;
only, as we left D., my sister caught a
glimpse of him seated in the shade of a
broad buttress of the cathedral, listening
to a shrill sweet *cantique* that was being
sung in the "ragged school."

PART VII

"Try what repentance can; what can it not?"—*Hamlet*.

"Four things that are not in Thy treasury
 I bring to Thee, O Lord !
 My nothingness, my wants,
 My sins, and my contrition."—*Persian Poem*.

Growth in repentance—No easy task—The "pearl" among Christian graces— Why this comparison holds good? — Self-examination a rugged duty — How best carried out—" Ghostly counsel"—Valuable when honestly asked—And acted upon—Conscience-money—An instance of restitution.

SINCE there is not a just man on earth that doeth good and sinneth not, the most loyally obedient must still stand in need of repentance. "Repentance whereby we forsake sin," as our catechism so tersely and well describes it.

If the emerald is the emblem of hope,

and the sapphire of heavenly-mindedness, may not the pearl with purest ray serene, free from glitter and glare, be likened to the grace of repentance? There is a special fitness in this, if what naturalists tell us of the origin of the pearl be true. Grains of sand or grit are apt to work their way out of an unquiet sea into the pearl-oyster shell. The creature in its efforts to expel them, emits a substance resembling the "*nacre*" of which her shell is made. This runs and hardens into the globe-shaped things we call pearls, and the concentric layers of which each pearl is composed cause that wonderful and lovely translucency which jewellers call "water." Thus repentance, like the pearl, is born of a persistent struggle to expel evil, and, amid stormy and unfriendly influences without, to recover and to keep purity within.

The pearl is formed in the seclusion of the closed shell adhering immovably to the living rock.   Neither its .shape nor its delicate brightness could exist were the shell tossed to and fro, open to passing waves.   Thus repentance cannot grow in a distracted heart, nor in a life of continual self-chosen hurry and bustle. "Commune with your own heart and in your chamber, and be still ;" are not these inspired words like early dew, or the morning breeze, to a soul parched by "earth's sun and dust"?   They naturally lead us to the subject of self-examination, and the danger of neglecting it in these breathless days.   Daily, if possible ; at the least weekly ; and always before approaching Holy Communion; ought we, even the youngest amongst us, to look narrowly into our own hearts, if we would honestly and thoroughly try to expel thence the grit of selfishness, covetousness, or bitterness.

This caution is absolutely necessary in these days, when the Holy Eucharist is in many places so easy of access, that not a few young persons rush to the altar-steps from ball or opera, giving themselves no leisure for devotional thought, either beforehand or later on in the sacred day. The man who irreverently stretched out his hand and touched the ark of God was smitten for his error ; is it safe for us to trifle with our ark ?

These and other evils would be cut up at the roots by honest self-examination. Therefore, we cannot exert our influence better than by pressing the claim of this rugged duty. " *C'est le premier pas qui coute.*" Beginners are so often quite puzzled how to set about it, that it is a real kindness to have some plan to suggest. The experience of elder people will generally be able to suggest some manuals which have helped themselves, and which, if clear, pithy, practical, and not too suggestive of evil, must help others. Where leisure is small the five clauses of the last answer in the Church catechism will furnish a

useful clue ; where time is not stinted, the
eight Beatitudes, or the Ten Commandments, read in the light of the Sermon on
the Mount, have given valuable aid to the
conscience.   Divine words must be safer
guides than human words, they go so
straight to the heart—its hidden idols, its
pride, and self-satisfaction.   An instance
of the unaffected humility produced in
one of the holiest of men by rigid self-
inquiry is fresh in my memory.   We all
know how the beloved Bishop Selwyn
went out with his life in his hand, and
toiled many years in New Zealand and
Melanesia, and laid the foundations of the
Gospel-kingdom deep and strong, amid
savages and cannibals.   If any man had
whereof to boast, it was he.   So far from
this, in a sermon preached not long before
his death, he spoke thus : " Which of us,
looking to the good which we might have
done to souls, and comparing it with the
good which we *have* done, which of us, I

say, but must pray, 'Deliver me from blood-guiltiness, O God'?" The bishop's whole heart seemed to go forth in these words. They may well show us what a very earnest and serious business repentance ought to be, and rebuke such of us as fail to avail ourselves of Lenten and other like seasons for this great heart-work.

Those who, in moments of utter perplexity, either cannot "cleanse the bosom of the perilous stuff" that loads it, or cannot decide on the right line of action, are, as we all know, advised in our Prayer-book to resort to some holy and experienced minister of God for counsel and help. Many a lad driven from home into some strange city in order to earn his bread has had cause to bless such help in his need : many have suffered loss from refusing to seek it, or, alas, from not having it to turn to. In the rare case of young wives and daughters needing more individual guidance than husband, parent, or sponsor, Bible or Prayer-book, can supply, the same resource is open to them; but they need to be careful that it is an honest craving for practical counsel that actuates them, not an indolent wish to throw off their responsibilities on another, still less a morbid desire to talk about themselves, and to describe their real or supposed trials and feelings. This is a temptation to many feminine minds, as none know better than those wise spiritual guides whose difficult task it is to repress it.

Sin forsaken, good followed, restitution made—these are the fruits of repentance. It sometimes involves humiliating confession to those we have wronged, always shame and sorrow towards God; such shame, such sorrow, as a little child feels when conscience pricks, and it hides its tearful face and flushed cheek on a father's breast. "True joy is born of such sorrow," said Charles Kingsley.

In our climate, and with our calmer
temperaments, penitence, true and deep,
is mostly undemonstrative towards man :
of its dealings with heaven we can know
nothing save by their results : so we are
sometimes inclined in reading the lives of
holy persons of other communions and
climes to be shocked by, or distrustful of,
their open and fervent expressions of grief
and self-abhorrence, their vigils and their
austerities.   Where merit is claimed for
these, the good in them is, of course,
neutralised ; but more often they are the
tokens of genuine anguish, rather to be
taken pattern by in spirit, though not in
letter, than to be criticised or scorned.

How much of remorse, and how many
stings of self-accusation are represented
by those notices we often see in the
papers, headed " Conscience-money."   One
loves to believe that the good Spirit has
pleaded successfully with those erring ones,
and that, after making the sacrifices which

restitution involves, many a sorely-tempted man has laid his head on his pillow with a peace unknown for years.

There was lately a young tradesman resident in one of our northern towns, and carrying on a flourishing business there; he was grave and careworn for his years, and not sociable with his equals; he frequented church and seemed to hang on the vicar's words, though shy and reticent when they met elsewhere. One day he brought home a bride, apparently somewhat above him in the social scale. Still the cloud was on his brow, though his love and his pride in her could not be doubted. One winter evening there was a tap at the back-door of the vicarage, and Brooke was introduced into the vicar's study. His air of extreme agitation and distress struck the clergyman with surprise. For a while he could not command his utterance, but at last with trembling hand he held out some bank-notes, and begged the vicar to remit them to a former employer, whose address he gave. A conversation followed in which he pleaded guilty to repeated frauds in past years, now deeply repented of; and for which he desired to make restitution by instalments. On one point only did he hold out against the vicar's strenuous injunctions; the bare idea of telling his wife threw him into an agony, and he rushed away exclaiming; "I cannot, I cannot; she would despise, she would hate me!" Months of growing wretchedness were the results of this concealment, for the young wife soon found out that a secret was kept from her, and a considerable share of her husband's earnings was not allowed to pass through her hands; but in a happy moment, she too went to seek counsel from the fatherly vicar. By his means the barrier between husband and wife was broken down. Though deeply shocked, she forgave all, and their hearts came together again, wiser if sadder, than heretofore.

"Sorrow for sin," says St. Chrysostom, "is the sorrow which brings with it the most direct blessing; sorrow for lost riches does not bring them back; sorrow for the departed does not raise him up; sorrow for sickness does not cure, but rather increase it; but sorrow for sin brings health and life to the soul."

PART VIII.

"Ask her for milk, she will give you cream ; ask her for cream, she will give you the cow."—*Breton Legend.*

Generosity of spirit—In giving and forgiving—In helping the oppressed—Generous trait in a child—Instance of a generous impulse—Mere impulse wears out—Generous forbearance of Mr. T.—Matured generosity—Perfect forgiveness difficult—Every fibre of ill-will to be torn up.

WE pass on to generosity, to giving and forgiving. The dawn of life often shows such fair gleams ; generosity peeps out early, especially with boys ; it was a noble impulse that moved a very gentle boy, barely three years old, to struggle from his nurse's grasp in the Alexandrian massacre. He saw an English gentleman, who had been kind to him, brought in bleeding and wounded ; love conquered

K

fear as the child cried out, "They have hurted my Mr. C.! let me run and beat them."

This same virtue of generous daring often shines bright to the end of life, as in the case of the gallant sailor who having saved forty lives, was last year, at the age of eighty-two, still able and eager to go out with the lifeboat. What an enduring of hardness must the whole career of this noble fellow have been! In contrast with this trait is one of a generous and good-natured impulse which once saved a poor soldier from condign punishment. I tell you the story as an old Peninsular officer told it me. One hot summer during the Peninsular War much fatal sickness visited some of our regiments owing to their eating very freely of the wild honey found abundantly in the woods of Central Spain. Lord Wellington, being on the spot, issued strict orders that no more honey was to be taken under the severest penalties. One evening he was on the edge of a wood with some of his staff, when a soldier emerged from among the trees with bent head, staggering under the weight of a hive of honey. The man had chopped off that part of the tree-trunk in which the bees had built, and was carrying it on his head like a helmet, the lower part of the dripping bark concealing his forehead and eyes completely. "What have you got there?" asked Lord Wellington. "Honey!" cried the soldier, all unconscious to whom he was speaking; "we are going to cut it up, and you shall be welcome to as much as you like!" "Hang the fellow," said Lord Wellington to his staff, "I can't be hard upon him after that," and he passed on.

This open-hearted soldier may serve to represent the popular notion of generosity, as an effervescing emotional quality, proper to the young, who feel acutely, but are not

given to thinking, far less to calculating
and balancing one claim against another.
Moreover, it is rather supposed to have
exhaled itself, and spent its force, by the
time we reach middle life—and so it does,
if derived from impulse only; for I suppose
every one has observed how parsimonious
people sometimes grow, who have in youth
spent lavishly on themselves and others;
and how sour and intolerant people sometimes become, whose open-hearted confidence has been unwisely given and therefore abused.   But we are not put into the
world to deteriorate thus.   No, we are
meant year by year to feel, and speak, and
act, and, above all, forgive, more generously
and fully to the end of the chapter.   As
fruits mellow, so must we.   As sweet grass
turns into sweeter hay under the warm rays
of the sun, so must we breathe out to the
sun of our souls the fragrance of matured
generosity and forgivingness.

Such was the conduct of the patriarch

Abraham, when, in advancing age, he gave to his nephew a full and free choice as to where he would settle, content to come off second - best himself. The princely Jonathan, heir to Saul's kingdom, was full fifty years old when he said to the brother-in-law, whom he loved as his own soul, " Fear not, thou shalt be king, and I shall be next after thee." It is " Paul the aged " who pleads for Onesimus with such touching and delicate generosity, writing with his own hand to Philemon, " If he owe thee aught, put it to my account ; I will repay thee." So divine is the Scriptural record that the lapse of ages does not make these traits one whit less fitted to serve as models for us.

Where the habit of mind is generous and forgiving, a hundred opportunities for exercising it will spring up. An old friend of ours justly prided himself on the possession of fine Indian china, specially of two noble jars which stood in his hall.

One sultry summer day a poor man had walked several miles to speak to him on business, and, being overcome by the heat, fell heavily across one of the jars, shattering it to pieces. The owner, hearing a crash, rushed to the spot, as did one of his servants. There was a momentary pause of dismay, then Mr. T. said gently, " Let us carry the poor fellow out of the room before he recovers consciousness ; and on no account let him know what he has done."

I believe we have not a few amongst us of whom it might still be said, " If you would secure his good offices do him a wrong." Most clergymen have witnessed something of the heroic patience and forgiveness with which many a wife, or young son or daughter, bears taunts, privations, ill-usage, from the hands of a husband or father given to intoxication. But such struggle and endurance, from their very nature, are shrouded, as far as may be, from the cold gaze of outsiders. Their "Father who seeth in secret shall reward them openly."

I suppose moralists are not far wrong when they tell us that to forgive out and out is the hardest thing in the world. Perhaps some of us have experienced how, when one thinks complacently that one has rooted up a grudge from the ground of the heart, some slight fibre of it will remain behind, and betray itself by a depreciating remark respecting the person that has annoyed us, or by a horrid little feeling of satisfaction at hearing him depreciated by another. Happy for us if the perception of the meanness startles us, while yet young and of vigorous mind, into a thorough sifting of the soil and eradication of the ugly weed.

PART IX.

" The end crowns all."—*Shakespeare.*

Growth in patience—Egyptian " Book of the Dead"—Egyptian thought as to a future state—Christian view of it—Gradual detachment from present things—Cheerful devolving of work on younger shoulders—Growing infirmities accepted—Details—Services gratefully received, even when awkwardly offered—Beware of fastidiousness—Preparations for death of two eminent laymen.

IN an excellent book, Keary's *Nations Around*, and also in a recently published work on Egypt by Mr. Villiers Stuart, there are very striking and solemn extracts from the old, old *Book of the Dead*, embodying the belief of the Egyptians in a state after death, called by them the passage into the under world. These traditions respecting departed souls are brought very near to us when we read of the bodies, which clothed them thirty centuries ago, lying undecayed, with the necklaces of natural flowers, blue larkspur, yellow mimosa, budding lotus, which loving hands laid over them, still preserving form and colour.[1]

This *Book of the Dead* describes, in words that remind us of Dante, the entrance of the newly-freed soul into the dusky atmosphere of the under world; its wanderings in a region half gloom, half light, not trackless, but leading, under the escort of "human-headed hawks," and such-like emblematic beings, to the hall of perfect justice. There sits Osiris, lord of truth, and there stand the forty-two assessors of the dead; each narrowly catechises him as to one special sin, and happy the soul that could reply: "I have not banished God from my heart; I have made none to weep; I have not

---

[1] Mr. Stuart saw a wasp, dried up but perfect, which, doubtless attracted by the flowers, had shared the entombment of Amunoph I. at Thebes.

stolen, neither told lies; I have not wasted time; I have not talked at random; I have not praised my own sayings; I have turned no water-course; I am pure! I am pure! I am pure!" To such an one the "gates of the meek-hearted" fly open, admitting him into the city of truth; while such as have wasted their time of probation in the body are led away by a path ending in thick darkness.

Thus the true Light, which lighteth every man, left Himself not without witness in the hearts of thoughtful Egyptians, granting them a glimmer of "righteousness, temperance, and judgment to come." Formidable must the prospect of this last have been, for even the untaught intellect can scarcely think of its Maker as being "such an one as itself"; and imperfection must needs quail before perfection. This brings us back to our own position as years advance and the moment draws near when we too must stand before the Lord of Truth. Not, thank God, on our own merits shall we stand there, but on His who made "a full, perfect, and sufficient sacrifice, oblation, and satisfaction for the sins of the whole world." I remember to this day, with a glow of comfort, the emphasis with which Dean Stanley, preaching in Westminster Abbey at a time when controversy ran high, gave in his adhesion to these words, which do indeed contain all our salvation and all our desire. None the less, as proof of adoring thankfulness, does the Lord of Truth expect good fruit from us. How can we best get this fruit to ripen under the shadow of the sere and yellow leaf?

First, then, as soon as we feel within ourselves a distinct lessening of strength and of vital energy, it would be well to begin transferring our work by degrees to younger shoulders. If we are wise, we shall have prepared and trained the shoulders for it; and, having devolved our

work frankly and cheerfully, we must see
that no jealousy, no hankering after lost
power, no asperity if new methods are
tried, and especially if they succeed, rankles
within us.   Many of us must have observed a sudden collapse of good and
useful work, simply because the hand that
guided it singly has been paralysed, and
there is no one to take it up.   The same
thing holds good in family life.   Surely
every mother ought to admit her girls to
some share in household management, or,
at least, knowledge of it.   For want of
this how many pitiably ignorant young
wives there are, whose dinners must contrast painfully in the husband's mind with
the luxurious repasts his club has accustomed him to expect, and who, through
sheer want of consideration, are capable
of putting a guest into a damp bed !   So,
like mercy, this graceful willingness to
share, and in due season to resign, the
reins of government is " twice blessed ;

it blesses him that gives, and him that takes;"—the latter with a sense of usefulness and helpfulness, the former with the joy of well-earned rest. And if the old and often misapplied saying, " Better wear out than rust out," should be quoted against us, we may reply, " Repose is not necessarily sloth ; time given to thought, to meditation, to intercession, may bear as rich fruit as that given to toil." The bee that waits at the hive door and relieves his fellows of their honey-freight, and patiently stores it, is as useful as the bee that flits and sucks from blossom to blossom. Of the old it may truly be said, " Their strength is to sit still;" and many a bed-ridden or sofa-ridden invalid is the loved and revered referee of old and young in the home *coterie*.[1]

Secondly, it is one thing to meet trouble half-way by keeping a morbid look-out

[1] There are beautiful thoughts on this subject in Miss Yonge's *Womankind*.

for it, and quite another so to arm ourselves for suffering as not to count it a
strange thing when it comes.   A right
view of our position as " sinners in a life
of care " is, of course, our best preparation ;
and next to that comes a pitying practical
acquaintance with sickness in its hospital,
or workhouse, or cottage aspect.   Go
round the wards of the best-managed
infirmary or union, and see many in the
prime of life so crippled by rheumatism,
or weakened by disease, as to have scarcely
a hope left of ever earning their own
bread or their children's bread again ;
mark the trustful patience, the quiet sub-
mission with which not a few of them bow
to the will of God ; and you will find in
the survey a strong rebuke of your own
impatience amid the abundance of your
creature comforts and in the enjoyment of
a settled income which saves all anxiety
for the future of those you love.

It is not always easy in chronic ailment

or infirmity to be equable and gentle with those around us, to " drink our wormwood with a smile,"—nay, even to bear in silence the rustle of our friend's news-paper, or the creaking of his shoes. Kind offices are clumsily performed, or a well-meaning visitor moves about us with loud whispers and on mysterious tiptoe, or stands regarding us with sad visage, when all the while it is a cheery word or sunny smile we are craving after. In these and such like petty annoyances, as well as in severer trials, well will it be for us and for our nurses if we have long since learnt by heart the lessons of self-control-ling love ; well, also, if we can discern kind intentions, though not very cleverly carried into act. Such patience is not ordinarily a plant of rapid growth ; it will not, like Aaron's rod, bud and bloom and bear fruit in a day, except by miracle. Nevertheless, the most impatient spirit need not despair ; prayer can and does

work miracles still in the kingdom of
grace, especially where previous opportunities have been few and meagre.
Patience may be born of one great
struggle, and have its perfect work afterwards—

> "Then mercy on our failings, Lord,
>   Our sinking strength renew ;
> And when Thy sorrows visit us,
>   Oh send Thy patience too."

The loss of all church-going for months
or years is a bitter drop in the invalid's
cup; for we none of us know, till we lose
them, how cheerful are the associations
with our church path and chiming bells,
and the old friends who greet us in the
porch, to say nothing of the hallowed
services within.   These services happily
follow us to our sick-beds, and we shall
rejoice in them the more if we guard
ourselves from the growing fastidiousness
of our day, and do not allow a dialect, a
gaucherie, a homely bearing to interfere

with our comfort in receiving God's message of love from His authorised messenger.

In this important respect, as in many lesser ones, the indulged habit of picking and choosing what best gratifies our taste, instead of taking what seems our allotted portion, comes sadly against us in later life. A friend writes thus on this subject : " I remember, when I was young and very full of life and spirits, being sent by my mother to take a small gratuity to a poor woman. I stayed to have a little talk with her, and must have betrayed some touch of wilfulness, for her reply was a gentle reproof: 'Miss Annie, dear,' she said; 'you are just wanting to carve for yourself; but if you will only be content to take what God carves for you, you will be truly happy.'" This poor woman was at the time worn with grief, having lost all her children. Little did she guess how deep her wise words sank into the young listener's heart, nor what good fruit they would bear in after years.

Cowper's chronic invalid, who—

> " Gives us, in recitals of disease,
>   A doctor's trouble, but without the fees,"

is certainly a tiresome and somewhat ridiculous personage; but to those who possess a fair stock of patience he is less trying than the sick friend who broods in silence over his symptoms and his pains, putting by, and almost seeming to resent, any token of sympathy. Such reserve, relieving itself now and then by bursts of irritation, is a feature of some complaints. Is it possible to rise above it? I know not; but, as a dear friend once said to me, it has its uses. Such an one may prove the *anvil* on which the Christian patience, pity, sweetness of temper, of those who live with him are to be hammered out, and shaped, and fashioned, to their infinite gain, perhaps ultimately to his.

This is no manual for sickness, but simply

an attempt at helpful thoughts as to how best our decline of life may be made profitable to our juniors. Two more hints will suffice, taken down from the mouth of one peculiarly thoughtful and wise in his dealings with souls: " As you draw near the confines of this life, think habitually of those gone before as in a definite place, nearer than we to the Shepherd of our souls: let your hope of rejoining them be a definite hope." Secondly, " fix your daily thoughts not so much on death as on the reappearing of our Lord ; this is the truer, brighter, sounder view, and it is that which St. Paul and the other Apostles took, as you will find by a careful study of their Epistles."

A time will come, if we are spared so long, when the progress of decay seems all at once to accelerate. We feel and know that the valley of shadows is narrowing on either hand, as the rocks almost meet overhead, shutting out " blue air" and sunshine, and that but one way lies open before us now, and "we have not passed this way heretofore." The bravest heart may stand still for a moment at first realising this; it may, it must, throb with awe and fear for a while. "There's nae back-door in this boat," said the "puir Scotch body" storm-tossed on a landlocked lake; and we can understand and share her feeling. But (God be praised!) if we have humbly felt after Him and found Him, and loved His ways and work, He will not leave us comfortless. Lifelong experience has proved this in our own case and in that of many very dear to us, who, to borrow Jacob's pathetic words concerning his Rachel, have "died by us by the way." We were witnesses of their good Christian lives; we saw how carefully they set their house in order, so as best to ensure peace and goodwill to their survivors; and, when they entered into the valley, we walked by them as far as we might go, till the overshadowing cloud hid them from our sight. One veteran soldier of the Cross, as he left us, said, "Do not grieve for my pain; His rod and staff comfort me; the rod is as comforting as the staff"; and again, "It is all light!" Another breathed out, as he went up higher, "How beautiful is God!" The faithful tender nurse, who for seventy-one years had dwelt under our family roof, parted from us with the simple words, "The Lord is taking me home, dears, and I am quite happy." To these and to how many other weary combatants the promise has come true, "Even to your old age I am He, and even to hoar hairs I will carry you." So we have a stay and we are strong, and looking steadily on at the cloud that hides out our future, it is no longer dark; rays from Him who is the bright and morning Star stream through with more or less of

vividness, yet in each case casting a sufficient light on the dim path to guide the
pilgrim step by step to his rest.

I have permission to quote the following
words from a paper, written by the late Sir
Philip Grey-Egerton several years before
his death, containing instructions for his
funeral: " . . . I wish my funeral to be as
quiet as possible; . . . the bearers to be
selected from the garden and farm labourers,
each put into a suit of mourning," etc. He
orders that the church should not be hung
with black, and that no hatchment should
be placed on the house; for he adds, " I
trust in God's mercy through Jesus Christ
that the occasion may be one of rejoicing
rather than of mourning."   These words
come with power from a man who at home,
and for fifty years in the House of Commons,
served his country devotedly; who, moreover, took a foremost place in the ranks
of science. As one who knew him best
says, " His daily life was truly a daily

preparation for the life hereafter; his words may safely be quoted, for they were prompted by no mere sentiment, but were in accordance with his deeds."

Here is a brief sketch of the last hours of a great statesman and brilliant speaker, the late Lord Derby :—

"During his illness his well-worn Bible always lay at his bedside; it was the last thing he asked for before unconsciousness came on. I never knew any one who valued his Bible more" (a loving niece writes this), "and even as children we used to remark his great attention and reverence in church; when the lessons were read it was quite as if he were hearing them for the first time."

It was my privilege many years ago to spend several consecutive weeks under the same roof with this great man, and to enjoy listening to his brilliant wit and endless stores of information; but the most interesting recollection is that of the Sunday evenings, when it was his habit to pull out his Greek Testament, and carefully and reverently translate for my benefit a chapter out of one of St. Paul's Epistles.   I remember, too, the indignant flash with which he silenced a flippant remark made by a bystander on the sacred text.

PART X.

" He who hath found a fledged bird's nest can tell
   At first sight that the bird is flown ;
   But what fair dell or grove he sings in now,
   That is to him unknown."—*Vaughan.*

" *Sere and yellow leaf*" *in Hursley Vicarage—Patience
—Its perfect work—Letters from Mr. Keble—Mrs. Selwyn
and the present Bishop of Melanesia at Hursley,* 1861—
Mrs. Keble's illness, 1862—*His devotion to her—Acquiescence of both in God's will—Life of Bishop Wilson—Cattle-
plague—Hursley offertory—Last letter—*" *Might we but
be found worthy.*"

WHAT words can paint the charm and
touching beauty of the "sere and yellow
leaf" as seen, up to the year 1866, in
Hursley Vicarage?   Not genius only, but
goodness, refinement, playfulness—all met
in the beloved poet of the *Christian Year*
and in his devoted wife also.   Lifelong
friends have written their lives, and have

described their youth and prime fully and worthily. They have described also the gifted sister, Elizabeth Keble, who added such a charm to that home, till she faded away. I only knew them for fourteen years, in their autumn of life; but what do I not owe to their all but faultless examples, their love and helpful counsels? Therefore—

> "Let me, tho' poor,
>   Lay at their door
>   This one poor blossom."

In the year 1862 Mrs. Keble was at death's door for a while, and her health remained most fragile ever after; but she bore up with great spirit, and was her husband's true helpmate still by the sick-beds of the poor, and in Day and Sunday school. Those children can never forget the sweet face, with its soft, smiling eyes, and delicate flush on the cheek, as she taught them under the spreading, fragrant lime-trees in the churchyard.

Another vivid picture rises to memory
—that of Mr. Keble in his church, so
perfectly restored, or rather rebuilt, by the
proceeds of the *Christian Year*.   There
was no very noticeable ritual in the services, but such deep heart-reverence in
every movement and in every tone of
Mr. Keble's voice when officiating, such
earnest, loving, grave pleading in his un-
adorned sermons, that there was nothing
left for heart to desire.   All present, from
the refined and accomplished Sir William
Heathcote down to the somewhat stolid-
looking peasants in their linen frocks,
might take home some weighty truth.
So I thought, when listening, by Mrs.
Keble's side, from our places in the open
tower, surrounded by wall - tablets of
Richard Cromwell (Oliver's meek son),
and his family.

These recollections date from 1852
when a friendship, never interrupted, be-
gan and steadily grew year by year.   Mr.

Keble writes to me in Chester thus in September 1861 :—" It is very kind of you, with your old walls, and river, and mountain distances, to think of our woods—I hope they will do their best to be pretty when you come. I am hearing the sweetest of Jacobite music while I write, from two of my nieces ; it ALMOST makes me feel disloyal in my old age."

How playful are these words, written before the shadows of sickness and anxiety already alluded to fell on that pastoral home. They never cleared away ; but assuredly they were fairer and lovelier than any mere worldly sunshine, so rich was the glow of faith and hope that lighted them up.

It was somewhere about this time that the present Bishop of Melanesia, then an Eton boy, accompanied his mother to Hursley for a week. Mr. Keble seemed to grow younger himself while watching his light-hearted young guest as he bounded over hedge and ditch, closely followed by panting Rover, the house-dog. At quieter moments he studied the boy's character, and traced his resemblance to his father "the great bishop," as Mr. Keble loved to call him.

One morning that we found ourselves in a difficulty, owing to the loss of the key of a locked box, the dear vicar observed our dilemma, and cheerily said : "Call Johnnie Selwyn—there is nothing that Johnnie cannot do." The words seemed of happy augury.

Let me give you another letter or two:—

H. V., 9th April 1862.—"My very dear and kind friend, I do not know how to thank you for your too kind note. . . . To think of its having been the first of your writing after so serious an illness, and of my having been such an ungraciously longful time in acknowledging it. Charlotte is certainly a great deal

better than she was ; but the shock was so
very violent, though but for a short time,
that I suppose it must take a good while
for the frame to right itself properly (if so
be) again. The doctor has not said so ;
but I have a strong impression that if we
had had to send for our old medical friend
from Romsey, he could hardly have
arrived in time. How can I ever be
thankful enough that this attack, which
was unlike any former one, did not visit
us two or three years ago, before we had
a practitioner in the village on whom we
could depend. He proves, indeed, very
skilful and sympathising, and a most
desirable attendant in every way. . . . I
will add the morning's report :—Our doctor
has just been here, praising her pulse, and
recommending champagne; so we are what
one may call jolly ! Annie M. was here
to be confirmed and saw her godmamma ;
it was a nice day, and our church looked
very pretty ; and our bishop, both then

and on the Saturday at Ampfield, did give such fatherly advice in such fatherly tones that it did one's heart good. Dear C. sends you her kind love, and you are not to think of her as suffering, only she is weak. Be sure we remember you, graceless must we be if we did not, all good be with you.—Ever your affectionate friend, J. K."

Mr. Keble was now very busy writing the life of Bishop Wilson of Sodor and Man.

21st August 1862.—"This is not to draw a letter from you, for I know you ought to have all the rest you can get, every way; and my conscience almost smites me to think of your having written that kind, kind letter about C., when you were not fit to write at all; however, I must ask you to tell one of your charitable secretaries to say to me on your behalf, whether you have any objection to my printing in a note, of course anonymously, the paragraph which you kindly wrote to C., with the description of Burton church and village; I am 'ripe for asking' as the page is in proof; but I have told them to wait before they strike. I have very little of the picturesque, and every inch is valuable, and will give the book a better chance. · C. Y. is in Edinburgh; what a good thing for Edinburgh!"

This biography of Bishop Wilson was certainly a great refreshment to Mr. Keble's mind. He has told me how he loved to muse on the noble, upright character of the bishop, as tried by cruel persecution, and as illustrated by the beautiful prayers and maxims of his *Sacra Privata.* "It strengthens one," said Mr. Keble more than once, "to go on cheerfully in our own day of church trouble and rebuke."

In December 1863 Mr. Keble wrote thus: "I have not yet thanked you for your contributions towards the life of Bishop

Wilson (if such a thing should ever be written ; for I feel it has not been written yet, only materials gathered for it).   But one has a great satisfaction, as a sort of antiquary, in collecting these materials. Your information respecting the King's School (Chester) is very interesting.   One is glad to identify the places in which Tom Wilson scribbled, doubtless, and made blots, and kicked his heels, like other boys."

It was very sad in July 1865 to find one's self in the porch of the vicarage, and receive no welcome there, and find no loving hands outstretched in greeting. Both were ill ; he was much altered by his attack of paralysis, moved feebly, and lay on the sofa for hours each day ; and she looked thin and hectic and very failing; though always bright and cheerful with him.   She had not strength for reading aloud ; so we, their guests, shared that happy task.   I think poetry soothed and

attracted him most; perhaps it had
always done so; for I well recollect, at an
earlier date, the deep interest which he
took in the Idyll of *Guinevere*, in the
grand, tender, forgiveness of King Arthur;
while her repentance and cry for mercy
seemed a parable conveying higher mean-
ings to him. It was in gorgeous summer
weather that I last saw beloved Hursley,
and the friends who made it so dear.
The smell of jessamine or lime blossom,
with which the air was heavy, always
brings back those golden hours. How
patient Mr. Keble was! not a trace of
irritability—all thankfulness for his mercies,
and solicitude for " the dear wife," now so
evidently sinking. It had long been her
secret and submissive prayer that she might
live to tend and comfort him to the end;
but at that moment there seemed small hope
of it, for he was rallying and she was not;
but, as we all know, her heart's desire was
eventually not denied. In August a few

trembling lines from her pen announced the final move to Bournemouth.   One regretful mention of the garden escapes her, "it is so beautiful, so bright with flowers ;" but the whole tone of the letter is acquiescence and peace.

In January Mr. Keble writes : —
BOURNEMOUTH, 16*th Jan.* 1866 (he writes of his wife) : "She continues, as to pulse and appetite, much in the same state ; sometimes brightening up, and able to be moved for a short time into the sitting-room, then more sinking again. . . . I am in trouble about that bad spasm ; may God preserve her from it, if it be His will! but there is no mistaking her inward brightness through it all ; and it is marvellous how, even in the midst almost of her faintings, she manages to look after people's wants, and to wait upon those who are waiting on her. . . . On the whole, looking back, I cannot hide it from myself that she is gradually growing

weaker, and as George Herbert calls it, undressing; I do not ask the doctor, who is a friendly skilful man, about time; but try to live on from day to day; and she seems helped to look it all in the face. Her sister is with her, and Mrs. Y. with her son, and two trusty and loving servants; so her husband's many defects as a nurse are in some sort compensated, and what is left to him is mostly to watch her and learn from her what he ought to have learnt long since. God bless you for all your love to her. . . ."

Four more precious letters followed. In the last Mr. Keble having, it would appear, heard of the fatal cattle-plague, then ravaging the dairies of our county and city, wrote to me urgently for details on the subject; his sympathy and sorrow were quite overflowing and did our hearts good. I must plead guilty to having softened down the sad reality as far as possible in my reply, well knowing how those tender hearts would ache for us and for the poor suffering animals, whose moans were seldom out of our ears. Some traits of unselfish goodness I related, as of the honest old butterwoman who never would consent to raise her price, nor to make a harvest out of the troubles of others. He was interested, too, by the quaintly-worded sorrow for her nine beautiful cows of our own very honest but untaught milkwoman. "Ah, sir," she said to our clergyman, "if only I were prepared, glad would I be to die and go to my cows!" Seven hundred, out of the eight hundred cows which were lodged within the walls of Chester, died. Here is Mr. Keble's reply :—

"BOURNEMOUTH, 16th March 1866.

"MY VERY DEAR FRIEND—Our darling is still permitted to remain with us ; but her weakness, and I much fear her suffering, increases; so, if possible, do her calmness and sweetness. I sit and look at her till I wonder how it can ever

be that some whom I know are allowed to en-
tertain a hope of being with such an one in the
same home for ever.   But we are taught to
believe greater things than that, might we but be
found worthy !   I took the liberty, as I said I
should, of sending the contents of your precious
letter to Mr. Richards, to assist in making our
neighbours and parishioners understand the
amount of the distress.   The result I send
with this ; hoping you will kindly excuse the
trouble I give in asking you to apply the money,
in what way you think best, for the relief of
those who suffer by this severe judgment.   We
add £5 to the offertory.   In any account that
is kept please let the £8 : 10s. be referred to
the Hursley Offertory, and the £5 appear
anonymously.   Charlotte suggests that I should
send also our curate's letter, which I gladly do,
in justice to my good parishioners.

"We have still our three or four active
nurses—my sister from Bisley, her servant, and
our own Anne—my brother to keep me company, and Jem Young to wait on us all.   I do
not know, if she *was* to be ill, how we could be
much better provided for, *D. G.*

"The Richards's are leaving Hursley, and

I am seeking a curate. I have asked Mr.
Mountain, the late Bishop of Quebec's son;
he is in Canada, and I may have to wait long
for an answer. Can you name at once any
one whom you can thoroughly recommend
in case of his failing me? Now with C.'s
best love, and both our kind remembrances
to you all.—I am always, your grateful and
affectionate,

J. K."

The gentle close of those two lives is
known to all ; some of us know of the pain-
less peaceful wanderings in which he bade
the loved ones round him bring " more
lilies to deck the upper chamber," and of
the engraving of the Crucifixion that was
placed at the foot of his bed by Mrs.
Keble's desire, and carried back to her as
soon as he had breathed his last on that
solemn Maundy-Thursday. I learnt from
her sister how, on receiving back this
engraving, the wife (one could never
think of her as a widow) meekly whis-

pered something about " joyful tidings,"
and " that he would see his Saviour first."
On the eve of Ascension she followed
him.   We cannot wind up better than
with these touching examples of faith and
hope blooming amid decay.   May our
last moments be as peaceful ; or, if a more
painful struggle be ordered for us, and we
should feel consciousness and self-control
endangered, may we have grace to say
like Sir Jacob Astley on the battlefield :
" O Lord ! if I forget Thee do not Thou
forget me."

We have tried (however feebly) to look
closely into the heart's workings, both
at its first conscious entrance into life
and at its final exit, with the wish and
hope that these suggestions respecting
them may prove helpful to others.   When
that blessed day shall come in which
the Voice that breathed o'er Eden shall
be heard saying, " Behold I make all
things new " ; may the renewing touch

be in mercy vouchsafed to each one of us, obliterating every trace of mortal frailness, and recreating us, bright and fair, for the Paradise of God.

THE END.

Printed by R. & R. CLARK, *Edinburgh.*